KIAN UNLEASHED

BROTHERHOOD PROTECTORS WORLD

TEAM KOA: ALPHA
BOOK FIVE

KRIS NORRIS

Twisted Page Press LLC

To my fellow partners in crime. I'm so utterly thrilled and honored to be part of Team Koa with you amazing ladies. Here's to all the adventures we'll share throughout our journey.

And to Chris… the most incredibly giving and talented person I know.

BROTHERHOOD PROTECTORS

ORIGINAL SERIES BY ELLE JAMES

Brotherhood Protectors Series

Montana SEAL (#1)

Bride Protector SEAL (#2)

Montana D-Force (#3)

Cowboy D-Force (#4)

Montana Ranger (#5)

Montana Dog Soldier (#6)

Montana SEAL Daddy (#7)

Montana Ranger's Wedding Vow (#8)

Montana SEAL Undercover Daddy (#9)

Cape Cod SEAL Rescue (#10)

Montana SEAL Friendly Fire (#11)

Montana SEAL's Mail-Order Bride (#12)

SEAL Justice (#13)

Ranger Creed (#14)

Delta Force Rescue (#15)

Dog Days of Christmas (#16)

Montana Rescue (#17)

Montana Ranger Returns (#18)

BROTHERHOOD PROTECTORS WORLD

ORIGINAL SERIES BY ELLE JAMES

Brotherhood Protectors Hawaii World

Team Koa Alpha

Lane Unleashed - Regan Black

Harlan Unleashed - Stacey Wilk

Raider Unleashed - Lori Matthews

Waylen Unleashed - Jen Talty

Kian Unleashed - Kris Norris

Brotherhood Protectors Yellowstone World

Team Wolf

Guarding Harper - - Desiree Holt

Guarding Hannah - Delilah Devlin

Guarding Eris - Reina Torres

Guarding Payton - Jen Talty

Guarding Leah - Regan Black

Team Eagle

Booker's Mission - Kris Norris

Hunter's Mission - Kendall Talbot

Gunn's Mission - Delilah Devlin

Xavier's Mission - Lori Matthews

Wyatt's Mission - Jen Talty

Corbin's Mission - Jen Talty

Tyson's Mission - Delilah Devlin

Knox's Mission - Barb Han

Colton's Mission - Kendall Talbot

Walker's Mission - Kris Norris

Brotherhood Protectors Colorado World
Team Watchdog

Mason's Watch - Jen Talty

Asher's Watch - Leanne Tyler

Cruz's Watch - Stacey Wilk

Kent's Watch- Deanna L. Rowley

Ryder's Watch- Kris Norris

Team Raptor

Darius' Promise - Jen Talty

Simon's Promise - Leanne Tyler

Nash's Promise - Stacey Wilk

Spencer's Promise - Deanna L. Rowley

Logan's Promise - Kris Norris

Team Falco

Fighting for Esme - Jen Talty

Fighting for Charli - Leanne Tyler

Fighting for Tessa - Stacey Wilk

Fighting for Kora - Deanna L. Rowley

Fighting for Fiona - Kris Norris

Athena Project

Beck's Six - Desiree Holt

Victoria's Six - Delilah Devlin

Cygny's Six - Reina Torres

Fay's Six - Jen Talty

Melody's Six - Regan Black

Team Trojan

Defending Sophie - Desiree Holt

Defending Evangeline - Delilah Devlin

Defending Casey - Reina Torres

Defending Sparrow - Jen Talty

Defending Avery - Regan Black

KIAN UNLEASHED

BROTHERHOOD PROTECTORS WORLD

TEAM KOA: ALPHA
BOOK FIVE

KRIS NORRIS

"*Y*ou know, Kian, if you keep hanging out here by yourself, I'm going to start calling you, Waylen."

Kian Fox glanced to his right, flipping off one of his best friends and former teammates, Lane Benning, as the guy sauntered over, handing Kian a beer. "You're just sore because your lady friend turned you down." Kian elbowed Lane in the ribs. "Either you've lost your mojo, or you're still stuck on the mystery woman who made you late to the party."

Lane gave him a shove. "Shut up. There's no freaking mystery woman."

"Right, and Harlan's not over there, brooding, because Raider's teasing him about never having a one-night stand."

Lane looked over his shoulder, chuckling as

Harlan rolled his eyes at whatever their other buddy, Raider Torres had said. "Harlan makes it too damn easy. Though, he could loosen up a bit."

Lane motioned to the surroundings. "Even if this wasn't a party for the best CO we ever had, the ranch is impressive enough to warrant a pause."

"You know Harlan. He can't relax until he's talked someone down off the ledge. And with how much booze is going around, I'm not sure anyone's going to be sober enough to need an expert negotiator."

Lane laughed, again. Louder. "I love the guy like a brother, but damn... he's more serious than a heart attack. Speaking of which... Is that your paramedic bag tucked against the bar?"

Kian smiled. Of course, Lane had spotted his medic bag. Lane had been their resident sniper, and nothing slipped past the man. Which was why Kian found it amusing that Lane had all but chucked any form of schedule out the window since they'd all retired six months ago. Always arriving either early or late. Though, after all the years they'd spent planning every detail of a mission down to the second, Kian couldn't blame him.

He shrugged. "Drunk people have a tendency to need medical care. I'm simply being proactive. I like this shirt — I don't want to have to use it to stem the bleeding on some drunk sailor." He smoothed his hand down the front. "I just bought it."

"I can tell. It's very… umm…"

"Stylish? Sexy?" Kian winked at Lane, knowing it would irk the guy. "Awesome?"

"White. It's white and bright and clean. Like, ridiculously clean."

"Shut up."

"So, now's not the time to tell you about that barbecue stain…"

"Nice try, wise ass. But Raider already pulled that one on me, the bastard. Right after he tossed a rock my way yelling, frag out."

"He does have a unique sense of humor. But I'm sure we would, too, if we dealt with bombs all day. I don't care how much he claims it's the safest gig out there, the guy's nuts."

"I don't know… You're the one going on about me wearing a white shirt to a party."

"You brought your medic bag because you thought you'd have to deal with blood, which seems at odds with wearing white. Besides, you haven't voluntarily worn that color since that fiasco in Paris." Lane snorted. "I don't think an inch of your shirt was clean by the time you were done patching up that kid."

"Who tries to skateboard down several flights of stairs in nothing but a pair of shorts?"

Lane smiled, leaning back against the Tiki bar beside Kian. "Who knew old habits were so hard to break."

5

"You seem to be doing okay. Like I said. You were late. Again."

Lane grinned, but the tension around his mouth belied his apparent happiness. "We all have to do something to adjust. God knows we can't country hop from one adventure to another forever. Which reminds me… What do you think about Hawk and the Brotherhood Protectors?"

Kian glanced over at the man in question. Jace "Hawk" Hawkins. The guy in charge of the newest satellite branch of the Brotherhood Protectors. "He's an ex-SEAL, like us. That's all I need to know. And from what I've seen of the company, it's impressive. All ex-military personnel. State-of-the art gear. And this ranch…"

Kian whistled. "Not a bad place for an office. Probably doesn't hurt his wife's father owns the place."

He eyed Lane. "Should I be reading more into this?"

Lane waved it off. "Just thinking out loud. I know the others are getting antsy. Hard to step back off that ledge, ya know."

"Good thing we've got Harlan, then."

Lane spat his gulp of beer across the grass. "Jackass. I nearly choked. And the last thing I need is you giving me mouth-to-mouth in front of all the ladies."

"Please, I'm a great kisser."

"I'll take your word on that." He nodded at Raider and Harlan. "Looks like it's my turn to tease Harlan about how he'll be going home alone. Do me a favor and get Waylen to chill out and enjoy the party. He's been standing on the fringes for the past hour. He might listen to you."

Kian glanced at his best friend. While he considered all of his ex-teammates brothers, his connection with Waylen often had him wondering if they'd been separated at birth. One of those freaking twin things he'd read about. Because Waylen understood Kian in a way no one else ever had. Knew when he needed space or a firm kick in the ass. And Kian had that same sense about Waylen.

Like now. Just looking at how Waylen scanned the crowd, faking a smile when Harlan and Raider ambled over and started razzing him, Kian knew his buddy wasn't quite ready to chill and kick back the way Lane had suggested. Not that Kian was surprised. Ignoring the fact Waylen was their tech specialist — who often preferred tinkering with his gadgets over chatting it up with a group of people — he'd spent the first seventeen years of his life on the Big Island. Had been dragged away to Chesapeake Bay after his father had died from a sudden heart attack. Both of which meant this homecoming held a mixed bag of feelings for the man.

Though, even Kian had to admit Waylen was edgier than normal. Had been more than a bit preoccupied since they'd touched down at the Kona airport. And Kian had a nagging suspicion this went beyond the unhappy memories. That there were other ghosts haunting the man.

Kian made a mental note to ask his buddy once the party started winding down. Though, with everyone celebrating the retirement of one of the Navy's finest commanding officers, Glenn Gadsden, Kian doubted it would wrap up before the first rays of sunrise crested the horizon.

He took a moment to appreciate the stunning sunset — how the stars were just starting to poke holes in the reds and yellows that chased each other across the sky — when a subtle whop whop whop sounded above the band. He focused on the spot just beyond the trees, smiling at the helicopter lining up the helipad. It wasn't much. Just a small concrete square with perimeter lighting that was large enough to house the machine without disrupting the flow of the land or disturbing the party.

Though, with enough food to feed several platoons and an open bar, he doubted anything short of one of the volcanos blowing their top would stop the celebration.

He glanced at the horizon, the dark silhouettes like omens against the sky. Thankfully, all three had been quiet since they'd arrived, especially Kilauea — the most likely to put on a show — and Kian hoped it stayed that way. Ever since he'd lost his childhood home to a fire, he preferred not to get too close to any type of flame if he could avoid it, including mountains that spewed lava.

A gust of downwash had him focusing on the chopper, again, as it landed on the pad, the engine immediately spooling down. The rotors were still slowly circling the machine when the far door opened — a pair of dusty boots hitting the concrete a second later. Though, it was the long tanned legs and stunning silhouette that held his attention as the woman made her way around to his side, grabbing some boxes out of the back.

He swallowed, nearly choking on his own saliva because the woman was gorgeous. With sensuous curves, lean muscles and long auburn hair glowing like fire in the setting sun, she reminded him of the images of the goddess Pele hanging in the hotel. And based on how she carried herself, he didn't doubt she was just as fiery.

She must have sensed him staring because she froze, two boxes in her hands, her back to him. She didn't turn — didn't do anything other than stand there for several moments, her head slightly cocked toward him before placing the boxes on the ground then reaching for more.

He should go over — offer to help. Apologize for staring. Not that he'd been solely focused on her looks. Based on how she'd finessed the chopper onto the pad with minimal downwash and barely any sound, she obviously had the kind of skill he'd often witnessed in the military. And he couldn't help but wonder if she worked for Hawk, too. While the guy hadn't mentioned having a dedicated aviation department, it made sense.

Maybe Lane wasn't too far off in suggesting they take a closer look at what the Brotherhood Protectors had to offer because despite having horrible luck with any kind of past relationship, she was definitely the kind of woman he'd chance getting burned for.

A nudge to his shoulder had him spinning — nearly socking Waylen in the chest when his buddy seemingly appeared out of nowhere. Though, Kian had a feeling a bomb could have gone off and he would have been too preoccupied drooling over the pilot to notice.

He wiped his hand across his mouth, just to be sure, before shaking his head. "Jesus, buddy. Don't sneak up on me like that."

Waylen laughed. "I didn't sneak. I walked across the lawn."

"Well, next time make more noise. The band's got it cranked so high the ground's vibrating."

"It's not that loud. And I called your name." Waylen leaned in closer. "Twice."

Well, shit. Now Kian either had to out himself or make up a convincing lie. "I guess I got distracted admiring what Hawk's got going here."

It wasn't a *complete* lie. He *had* been wondering if the woman worked for Hawk.

"Can't argue with you there. She's a beauty. Is that a gardenia on her ass?"

"Say what?"

Kian snapped his gaze back to the helicopter, but the pilot was gone, nothing but a couple boxes stacked against the pop-out floats on the skid gear. Though, now that he wasn't laser-focused on the girl, he noticed the large white flower covering the rear section of the fuselage, along with the word *Huna* written in flowing script just below the mast.

Great. Waylen had obviously noticed him staring and was getting his kicks by stringing Kian along.

He scrubbed his hand down his face, taking a deep breath before eyeing Waylen. "As a matter of fact, it is."

"Maybe the pilot has one tattooed on her backside, too, because it was *her* ass you were staring at, right?"

"Well, it sure as hell wasn't yours." He took a breath — tried to get the woman off his mind. "You done being antisocial, or are you just taking a break so you can bust my balls?"

Waylen flipped him off. "I don't need a reason to do that. Besides, you know I don't like crowds."

"And I don't like volcanos, and yet, here I am, standing beside Hawai'i's most active one."

"It's easily forty miles away. Hardly right next door."

"Still…" He leaned against the bar, taking another swig. "So, what do you think about Hawk and his setup? Lane says the others are antsy to get back into the fray."

Waylen shrugged, though Kian didn't miss the tightness around his mouth. More of those ghosts, he'd been thinking about earlier. "It's definitely got potential. I know someone who works for the Montana branch, and he's got nothing but great things to say about the Brotherhood and the CEO, Hank Patterson."

"Is that a yes if you were given the chance to join?"

"Maybe. I…" Waylen sighed as he toed the grass, taking a long look around. "I guess I just never considered coming back here to stay."

And there it was. That haunted look in his eyes followed by an obvious shudder. The man was definitely hiding something.

Kian nudged his shoulder. "Which brings up my next point… Are you okay? Because you've been noticeably distant since—"

A loud rumble cut him off, the eerie sound vibrating through the earth and into his chest, much like the music had. Only this was louder. Stronger. More like a growl from somewhere deep below him.

The low resonance shaking anything not nailed down.

Earthquake.

Though, compared to the ones that regularly rattled through his hometown of Anchorage, Alaska, this seemed fairly tame. More of a suggestion of a quake than something that would do any damage.

Until the next one hit.

That one...

The sheer force nearly knocked Kian on his ass as Waylen grabbed his arm — steadied him. The band cut off, a hushed gasp rippling through the crowd as everyone turned to stare at those ominous silhouettes behind them.

Kilauea.

Only, she wan't quiet, now.

Smoke and ash billowed across the violet sky, bleeding all that color into an eerie gray while a crimson glow brightened the growing darkness. What Kian assumed was lava shooting out the top or maybe bubbling over the sides. Regardless, the incredible display sent a deafening silence across the yard.

He gained his balance, shaking his head as more tremors rumbled underfoot. He grabbed his medic bag, then glanced over at the chopper, ready to lend a hand if the pilot had returned and gotten knocked over from the quakes, but the area was still empty. Just those boxes now overturned onto the cement.

He sighed, focusing on the ever-increasing cloud as he held out his hand. "And there goes one of the volcanos, which means you owe me fifty bucks."

Waylen scoffed. "For what?"

"You promised me this would be a lava-free vacation, remember? Said, and I quote, 'Mauna Loa and Kilauea are sleeping. You'll be fine'."

"You are fine, jackass, and I can't help it if one of the damn volcanos decides to erupt."

"A bet's a bet."

Waylen grumbled as he reached for his wallet, handing Kian a fifty-dollar bill. "No one likes a sore winner, buddy."

Kian grinned, shoving the money in his pocket. "Don't get mad at me because you chose poorly. You should know better than to bet on something you can't control."

"I read the reports. Neither of them were supposed to erupt anytime soon. Though, this new development does complicate things. I think we should find the others."

Kalea, Hawk's wife, was going through the various safety information and trying to keep the guests calm as Kian and Waylen crossed the yard — met up with the rest of their team. They were just discussing their next move, when Lane spotted Hawk and his crew heading for their office in one of the outbuildings behind the house. What looked like a full-scale rescue mission in the making.

A collective nod, and Kian and the others were charging ahead — offering their services, as Hawk ushered them into the office. He launched a map of the island onto one of the monitors just as the radio sparked to life, the first calls for help already coming in.

It didn't take long to thin the numbers as Hawk handed out assignments. Lane was the first of Kian's group to bolt out the door, volunteering to help a woman with a suspected child abduction. Raider and Harlan went next, heading to towns at risk of getting cut off. Twenty minutes into the eruption and only Kian and Waylen were left.

Waylen muttered something under his breath, leaning toward Kian. "Now, I'm getting flashbacks to middle school and always being picked last."

"Shut up. Hawk's just going in order. Maybe he wants the brainy guy to stay behind?"

"So, why are you still here, then?"

"So I can treat your wounds once I kick your ass."

Hawk cleared his throat, eyeing them as he cracked a smile. "You lovebirds done cooing at each other, or should I find someone else to take this call?"

Waylen rolled his eyes as he flipped Kian off. "Where do you need us?"

"In the air, actually. We've got a request for an aerial account of where the lava's heading and how the ash and smoke are impacting the towns and areas both along the south coast and over to the west." Hawk handed them each a camera, nodding at Waylen. "These have multiple video capabilities. Benning told me you're the tech guy, so, I'll assume you can figure it all out. If you can capture as much data as possible, it'll help prioritize which areas need resources, first. Give the geologists some critical real-time data."

Waylen turned his camera over his hands. "I'm guessing you've got us a ride?"

"We deal with a local pilot by the name of Blake Garrett. Haven't found a job she can't handle, yet, including some pretty hardcore rescue calls. The lady's a spitfire. If you hurry, you'll catch her before she takes off. She'll need to circle the volcano, then head south as she makes her way back to Waikoloa. The deputy chief will have an officer waiting at the landing pad she's renting near the resort to take those cameras from you so he can get them to the resident geologists for recommendations. If she's feeling generous, Blake might even fly you guys back, though I'll be sure to have your rental returned if you get stuck."

"Are you sure she's okay to fly in this?"

"She's night and instrument rated and hands down one of the best pilots I've ever met. If I didn't

know any better, I'd bet my ass she was ex-military."
Hawk gave Waylen a light shove. "Don't worry.
She's topnotch. And her helicopter's loaded."

Waylen nodded, holding the door open for Kian
to dodge through.

Kian looked at the camera, shaking his head.
"Seriously? Out of all the assignments, we get the
one that has us circling an active volcano? You
planned this, didn't you?"

"Don't be an ass. You'll be fine."

"If we die a fiery death, I'm so haunting you for
the rest of your life."

"You can't haunt me if I'm dead, too, Einstein.
Come on, before your flower girl takes off."

Kian gave his friend a shove, following him back
across the lawn and over to the helicopter. Blake was
packing supplies into the passenger seat when they
reached the helipad, what looked like a military spec
helmet resting on the controls.

Hadn't Hawk commented about how he'd
suspected she was ex-military? Though, he'd
phrased it as if he knew she wasn't. But judging by
the extensive instrument panel and the hoist
hanging off the side of the bird, it didn't seem like
a tour chopper. In fact, it looked more like the
machines he'd ridden in while in the Teams, with
harnesses in the back — high grade headsets
resting on the seats. Not to mention what he
assumed was a collapsed basket tucked under the

seats. Everything for those rescue calls Hawk had mentioned.

She didn't even look up, arranging some of the boxes as she talked over her shoulder. "I get all you military types love a good rush, but I promise you... Touring an active volcano never turns out the way you think it will. You'll get a pretty decent show just watching from the yard."

Waylen smirked. "We aren't looking for a tour, Ms. Garrett. Hawk sent us."

Blake stopped fiddling with the last box, pausing to glance at them. And damn, she was beyond stunning. With big blue eyes, symmetrical features and hair a few shades deeper than the red burning a line along the horizon, she had the kind of beauty men crossed the room for.

She arched a brow, giving them both a once-over. "Jace Hawkins sent you?"

"Yes, ma'am. Said you might be willing to lend a hand."

Blake crossed her arms over her chest, looking less than impressed. "Pretty sure I know all of Hawk's men, and I know I've never seen you two before."

Kian stepped up, doing his best not to smile like a giddy teenager. "We don't officially work for the Brotherhood Protectors. At least, not yet. We've only been retired from the Teams for a few months. We're here for our ex-CO's party, but I assure you, we're more than qualified for this kind of emergency."

"You dealt with active volcanos while in the service? Didn't realize the Navy had that kind of division."

He chuckled. If he hadn't been crushing on her before, he definitely was now. "More along the lines of being adaptable. I can call Hawk if you need his verification, but the longer we wait…"

"The sketchier it gets. Trust me, I'm familiar with how Hawk seems to forget he's not the one doing the actual flying. Let me guess… We need to circle the damn volcano, avoiding lava spires and toxic gases, so you two can photograph everything before we head south and fly by a bunch of towns so you can do a risk assessment."

"Sounds about right." He inched closer, inhaling the subtle fruity scent from her skin. "If you think it's safe."

"Safe? It's already dark with the trade winds blowing smoke and ash south around the mountains and over toward the resorts. The exact path we need to take. But seeing as I doubt you'll find another pilot crazy enough to give it a try at this hour, I guess you're stuck with me."

She ran her fingers across her hair, biting at her lip. "But if I think the ash is going to ruin my engines…"

"Whatever you think, Ms. Garrett."

"No one calls me Ms. Garret. It's Blake." She pointed to the rear seats. "Hop in the back."

Kian held out his hand. "Thank you. And I'm Kian, and this is my buddy, Waylen."

She stared at his hand for a moment, looking as if she wasn't quite sure if it was safe to shake it, then slipped her palm against his, giving Waylen an odd raise of her brow. "You might want to wait until we actually make it to Waikoloa before you thank me, but you're welcome. Now, make sure you buckle up. This isn't going to be a pleasure tour."

2

This wasn't how she'd envisioned the night ending. And based on how much the wind had picked up — the amount of smoke and ash pouring out of the volcano — the situation would only get worse.

Blake Garrett placed the last box on the seat as her two passengers strapped themselves in. They'd obviously been in a helicopter before, though, being ex-military that wasn't a surprise.

The Teams...

That's what Kian had said. And with her father having dedicated his life to flying for the Navy right up until he was killed in action, she knew it meant they were ex-Special Forces. And while they hadn't specified which branch they'd served with, she bet her ass they'd been SEALs, just like Hawk. Especially if Gadsden had been their CO. Though, she supposed they could have been Delta Force, since it was one of the few teams that took recruits from other branches. Regardless, it meant they were hardcore. Had likely seen more action than all her former crew put together. Not that she'd been deployed into active combat the way they would have been, but she'd done several overseas tours as one of the Coast Guard's Tactical Law Enforcement Teams, or TACLET, and had more than a few harrowing flights under her belt.

She narrowed her gaze, eyeing the guy on the right. Waylen. The one with the same name as her friend, Presley Miles' catamaran. Which, in itself, was odd enough, but there was something about his eyes. The shape of his mouth. As if she'd seen him before.

She hadn't. At least, not that she remembered, and Blake prided herself in never forgetting a face — couldn't afford to when it might get her killed. And based on how handsome he was, she definitely would have remembered shaking his hand or even just seeing him across a room. Still, she couldn't quite shake the sense of deja-vu that prickled the hairs on the back of her neck.

Blake slid her attention to Kian. While she hadn't met him, either, he'd been following her movements, earlier. Just before the eruption. Not that he'd been conspicuous about it. More like idle curiosity. But she'd noticed. Had gotten an instant tightening in her gut that had put her on edge, like she did when anyone stared too long. Looked as if they were trying to place her. And she'd been left wondering if he was on the ranch for her and not Gadsden's retirement party. That maybe Henry Russo had finally tracked her down and sent a few hitmen her way. And based on how Kian and Waylen carried themselves — the fact their muscles had muscles — guns for hire was definitely a possibility. When they'd told her Hawk had sent them...

She'd had a moment of pure panic. Of wondering if maybe Hawk was part of the Russo crime syndicate, too. If he'd been playing her this entire time — some twisted version of a long con — waiting until she'd given him a hint of trust before sending Waylen and Kian to kill her. Which she realized was absurd, but after everything she'd been through over the past few years — having her career implode along with her life — a bit of increased paranoia was the least of her worries.

A byproduct, she supposed, of living in the shadows, never letting anyone get too close in case they were planning on putting a bullet between her eyes. Her lifelong penance for putting Henry Russo in maximum security and crippling the family's drug operation. What she'd needed in order to look at her own reflection without wanting to smash the mirror.

Kian must have felt her staring because he

looked up — smiled. And just like that, all those butterflies in her stomach started fluttering for another reason because the man was striking. Dirty blonde hair, bright blue eyes, with the kind of massive physique that stretched the sleeves of his white button down. She hadn't missed the edge of some kind of tribal tattoo peeking out at his chest. What looked like a bear or maybe just some abstract design.

Either way, it made her want to see the rest. Trace the lines with the tips of her fingers. Maybe follow-up with her tongue.

Blake gave herself a mental shake, securing her helmet before sliding into her seat as she buckled her harness. Obviously, the years of celibacy were getting to her. Not that she was surprised, especially with how gorgeous the man was. But now wasn't the time to get any crazy ideas. Do something rash like falling for the sexy sailor sitting in the back of her helicopter. While she was fairly confident he wasn't a mafia hitman, it didn't mean he was safe.

Who was she kidding? Safe didn't exist in her world, anymore, and the sooner she remembered that, the better.

The thought cooled the heat slowly curling along her skin, and she managed to get the helicopter airborne without crashing into the trees or part of the ranch. Which was a definite possibility with the smoke and ash eating away the starlight and the moon nowhere close to rising, yet. Not that it would have helped, being nothing more than a silver. But any source of light would have been welcomed.

Blake switched to her night vision visor. It wasn't as precise as the kind of goggles she'd seen Hawk's men carry — the tech she'd used in the Coast Guard before her life had gone in the crapper — but it amplified the light enough she could navigate without relying solely on her instruments. Though, the infra-red forward looking radar and the high resolution terrain mapping units were a godsend. What might be the difference between reaching the volcano instead of crashing some place.

She keyed up the mic, giving her guests a quick glance. "You boys got your headsets on? Can you hear me?"

A rasp of static crackled through her comms. "Roger that. Coming through five by five."

The fact she recognized Kian's voice was proof she needed to get her head checked because she didn't do romance. Couldn't afford to let anyone in with the never-ending threat of retaliation hanging over her head from the fallout of the trial. Becoming friends with Presley had been risky enough. Not that she didn't trust the other woman. She did. Presley Miles was as solid as they came. Would drop everything if Blake ever needed her. While she didn't know Blake's history — couldn't

without putting a bullseye on her back, too —
Presley knew Blake was running from something.
That it was dangerous for her to have her photo
taken or associate with too many people. And
Presley respected that. Went out of her way to help
Blake stay in the shadows.

Blake had tried to warn Presley — had told her
she was radioactive and could go critical at any
moment, taking Presley with her. But Presley wasn't
the kind of person to shy away from danger. And
after walking away from everyone Blake had ever
known — the career she'd spent a lifetime crafting
— she wasn't ashamed to admit, she'd needed the
friendship.

More static, then Kian's voice, again, and it was
just as sexy as before. A series of goosebumps
cascaded down her skin. "Now that we're up here, I
didn't realize there were so few light sources. You
still okay with this?"

Blake laughed, then hit the intercom. "It's a bit
late to worry about that. And I have a night vision
visor and instruments that help me navigate. Not
quite military spec, but they do the job."

More than did the job, if she was being honest.
In fact, it was as close as she could get to her old
Coast Guard configuration without actually having
a search and rescue helicopter. Broadcasting to
everyone she wasn't what she claimed to be.

"I guess that explains the helmet and the

impressive setup you have. Much more than other tour companies I've seen. Though, I guess it comes in handy whenever you're helping out Hawk and his men. The guy said he throws some pretty hardcore jobs your way."

He'd been wondering about her helmet? Why her helicopter wasn't standard fare?

True, not many pilots wore helmets other than military or police, but she couldn't chance anyone catching a glimpse of her. Which meant donning the bucket unless she was certain she wouldn't be around other people.

Taking it off at Gadsden's party had been a rash decision, but with Kilauea putting on a show, she'd hoped everyone would be too focused on the volcano to notice her. And after flying all day, she'd needed to feel a bit of cool air across her face.

Of course, she would have worn the helmet in this situation, regardless, especially with the real possibility the trip could end poorly. Mother Nature was unpredictable, and the fact Kilauea had erupted when everyone had thought it would be weeks or months before they saw any concrete activity from any of the volcanoes, case and point. She just hoped the ash and smoke stayed high enough she could sneak in beneath it — get that footage the guys needed. What could spell life or death for the people living in the impact zone. And with Kilauea not following her usual pattern...

"He's been very generous and kept me pretty busy. Hang tight. We've got a system moving in quicker than they predicted. It might get a bit bumpy before we even reach Kilauea."

She banked right, heading for the coast. If she followed the shoreline, her passengers could get footage of all the small towns in Kilauea's usual path before she snaked her way inland. They'd catch the rest on the trip south then west toward the resorts.

At least Presley should be fine out on the water. While the smoke and ash could play havoc with the weather patterns, her friend was a seasoned captain. And Blake had no doubts she'd be mooring the boat someplace safe if the fallout ramped up the storm system moving in.

Blake made a mental note to check-in before she shut down for the night — do a flyby if necessary — as she reached the water and started the sweeping pattern over toward the volcano. Waylen and Kian were talking in the back, just the occasional murmur reaching her. They'd obviously twisted their microphones away so they wouldn't activate automatically, and she couldn't help but wonder what the exchange was about. More of that paranoia she'd been thinking about earlier. If they really were there to kill her and had used Hawk's name as part of their ruse.

Of course, if they shot her while she was flying, they'd die, too, so…

And this was why Presley was her only friend. Blake couldn't stop obsessing long enough to let anyone else in. Sure, being suspicious kept her alive, but she'd taken it to a whole new level. One where it lived and breathed right there beside her. Some twisted voice in her head preventing her from ever truly moving on.

She snorted. Like she'd ever be able to move on before Henry Russo was dead. And the likelihood of that happening anytime soon was as bleak as her love life. Even behind bars, the man was seemingly untouchable.

Another reason to focus on her work. Flying had always been her passion, and she'd be damned if she let Russo take that away from her. Not when he'd taken everything else.

She lowered the aircraft, focusing on the shoreline before banking it right, again, and heading inland — following the road for a while. The guys must have finished their conversation because they were snapping photos and taking videos when she glanced over her shoulder at them. Completely immersed in their task.

Noting how sexy Kian looked as he twisted to get a better shot — a gap in his shirt giving her a better look at that gorgeous tattoo inked on the thick band of muscles across his chest — showcased that she really did need more sleep. Or more tequila. Because she knew better than to get distracted, and she had no doubts he'd be an incredible distraction.

A mental pep talk to remind herself she came with one hell of a warning label, and she had her head back in the game. Was weaving her way along the network of roads circling Kilauea. A number of subdivisions had popped up along the edge of the volcano, most of which would be at risk if she continued to erupt in the current direction.

She glanced at the men, again, keying up the comms. "You gents getting everything you need? I could get lower."

Kian looked at her, coughed, as if he'd forgotten how to swallow. "Call me crazy, but if you get any lower, we'll be skimming along the lava."

Blake managed not to laugh, but the look on his face — half wonder, half terror. He definitely wasn't impressed with his assignment. "First time with an erupting volcano?"

He laughed, though even she could tell it was forced. "That obvious?"

"An educated guess. You're not going to puke or anything, are you?"

He glared at Waylen when the guy chuckled, giving him a sharp elbow in his ribs. "I'm fine. Just not a fan of fire-breathing mountains."

"You and me, both. Give me an ocean rescue, any day."

Kian arched a brow a moment before she realized what she'd said. That the words had popped out before she'd had the sense to crush them. More proof that she needed to get her head out of her ass because she never let personal information like that slip.

Thankfully, he didn't call her on it or ask for details, electing to focus on taking more photos. Whispering something to Waylen.

She let the awkward silence suffocate the cabin, doing her best to cover as much area as she could before the fumes and heat started taking a toll. She was just about to key up the mic when it chirped in her head.

"Not to add to your already questionable opinion of me, but is everything still good? I can't help but notice it's getting hotter in here, not to mention bumpier."

Kian, and she didn't miss the slight waver in his voice. Not that he would back down. She had no doubts he'd die in a fiery blaze before he gave into fear or admitted defeat. But it was refreshing to think that beneath the training and never-say-die attitude she associated with most ex-special forces soldiers, Kian might have a softer side.

"The conditions aren't too bad, yet. And I really don't want to have to come back out if we don't get enough footage."

Kian snorted, clearly conveying that it would

take biblical intervention in order for him to venture back out. Not that she blamed him. It was hotter and bumpier, and if she wasn't careful, they could all suffer from hypoxia or other breathing problems if the oxygen levels got low from the carbon and sulfur dioxides.

Though, compared to some of the water rescues she'd performed over the years — the helicopter bombarded by wind and spray, the cresting waves making it nearly impossible to hold the chopper level — this wasn't as challenging. A fact that could change at any moment if the heat and gases created swirling drafts that threw ash and smoke her way.

She'd give it another ten minutes then swing south — head for the shore.

A sudden burst of static over her auxiliary radio caught her attention, and she turned up the volume against the intermittent call.

"Mayday, mayday, may... This is the Waylen, Waylen, Waylen. Call number bravo victor nin—"

Blake smacked the radio as it cut out, the ash most likely messing with the signal.

"Waylen. I've got an injured passenger who needs... hospital... dead in the water."

The message continued, half the words lost to the static, but Blake was already inputting the coordinates as she dialed in the beacon's frequency. From what she'd caught of Presley's message, the closest Coast Guard vessel was a good thirty minutes out, and Blake doubted there were any boats in the vicinity that could get to the distressed catamaran before more casualties piled up. Not with her friend's vessel unable to maneuver in the punishing waves.

Blake banked the chopper over — hard — dropping it lower as she pegged the speedometer to the max. She made a blanket call across the radio, broadcasting her intentions — that she was responding to the distress call — then did a mental check of her supplies. This wasn't a sightseeing tour or info-gathering mission, any longer. This was a full-scale rescue op and with her best friend's life on the line, she was determined to push the chopper to its limits.

The comms buzzed. "Blake? Everything okay? Are we in danger?" Kian, though he sounded far calmer than when he'd been talking about the volcano.

Blake activated the comms. "Everything's fine but there's a slight change in plans."

"What kind of change?"

"Before I go into any details, I need to know what you boys did in the service. And I'm really hoping it involved rescue swimming, otherwise this is going to be very awkward."

Kian snorted. "We're ex-SEALs, so I think we've got a bit of experience under our belts."

She knew she'd been right. "Finally, a surprise I

can get behind. I just received a mayday call from a boat that's dead in the water with at least one injured passenger onboard who requires airlifting to the nearest hospital. We're five minutes out. I'm going to need one of you in the water, and the other to stay with me to man the hoist. In case you hadn't noticed, I've got a rescue ladder and a collapsible basket under the middle front seat."

Sounds rose from the back as the men dragged out the supplies. She wasn't sure which one of them would be jumping, too focused on making it to the blip on her screen.

Under five minutes, and she was closing in on the Waylen off her left side — was keying up the mic, again. "I've got the boat in my sights. Once one of you is onboard, switch to channel twenty-four so we can communicate. You can open the doors, now. The wind's going to really kick us around, especially once you're hanging below. It'll be easier to jump using the ladder. Whoever's staying with me can let me know when your part-ner's fifteen feet off the water so I can hold her steady, but this isn't going to be pretty. Get ready, and whatever you do, don't drown."

3

$\mathcal{K}$ian stared at the woman, wondering who she really was because she seemed extremely well-versed in water rescue practices for a civilian chopper pilot. And there was the part where she'd casually mentioned how she'd take a water rescue over circling a volcano. What he suspected had been a mistake because she'd clammed up the moment it had slipped past her lips.

But those were questions he could ask once they were back on solid ground.

He reached over and unbuckled Waylen's harness.

His buddy glared at him. "What the fuck are you doing? I'm not jumping."

"They hell you aren't."

"I believe I did this the last time you and I were in the back of a chopper together."

Kian shook his head. Only Waylen would claim to keep track of that shit. Though, after the bombshell he'd just dropped during their conversation after the chopper had taken off about some woman named Presley and how he'd been stuck on her since he was seventeen, nothing shocked Kian, now.

He wouldn't lie. He was a bit butt hurt Waylen hadn't felt he could confide in him. That Kian wouldn't understand. He did. Not that he'd ever been that hung up on a woman he couldn't let it go. But he knew about demons. Had enough of them whispering in his ear that he got the reasoning behind it.

Still, he couldn't let that kind of bro-code violation go unanswered.

Kian gripped Waylen's shirt and grinned. "Then, consider this payback for not telling me about this Presley woman you've been pinning over for twenty-three years."

"You're a fucking asshole, you know that."

"Been called worse. Let me know when you're ready to jump, and I'll tell Blake to hold it steady."

"Funny how she's so water rescue savvy all of a sudden. Makes me wonder what she's hiding."

"Me, too." He braced against the sudden surge of wind as he opened the doors and kicked out the ladder. "Now go, before I give you a shove."

"You so owe me…"

Kian merely smiled, helping Waylen onto the ladder then monitoring his progress as the man slowly inched down the rungs. It took about a minute before he was giving Kian the thumbs up.

Kian twisted the mic back next to his chin. "Waylen's at fifteen feet, Blake."

"Roger."

Blake's voice echoed through Kian's headset, far calmer than he'd predicted. Even if she had done a handful of these in the past, he'd expected a slight waver in her voice. The pitch higher or lower than normal. Instead, she was as cool as the water cresting below them. Had that chopper nailed in place, despite the rolling swells and gusting winds.

He'd bet his ass there was far more to the woman than she'd let on. That military connection Hawk had mentioned.

Waylen gave one last hand signal then dropped, free falling for all of two seconds before hitting the surface and plunging beneath the waves.

Kian started counting. Waylen was one of the best SEALs he'd ever had the pleasure to serve with, but even he couldn't hold his breath indefinitely. Kian would give the guy a full minute before he told Blake to get them insanely low so he could jump straight out the back.

Seeing Waylen's head bob out of the water twenty seconds later eased the tight feeling in his chest. Not because he'd been worried. He'd simply thought he'd left this kind of danger behind. And there was nothing he hated more than feeling helpless. With no comms systems — hell, no lifejackets — all he could do was mentally will Waylen the thirty feet over to the boat. And with the seas frothing like a rabid dog — the boat tipping in every direction like a damn bobblehead — drowning was definitely still on the table. Even for a professional swimmer like Waylen.

Time dragged by as Waylen headed for the stern, finally making his way on deck before disappearing inside. Kian's cue to ready the basket and get his medic bag open. He had the unit locked and hooked up with his supplies arranged across the seats when his headset chirped.

"So, Kian. Was that a medic bag I saw you carrying, earlier?"

He smiled. "I hadn't realized you'd noticed."

She shrugged, cursing a bit when a strong gust shoved the machine over — nearly knocked him on his ass. "I like to keep track of my surroundings. What kind of medic were you?"

"Rescue combat. There's not much I haven't seen or treated. Though, every team member knows some advanced first aid."

"That's reassuring. Were you able to get the basket hooked up or do you need instructions?"

"Locked and loaded."

That got him a stunning smile over her shoulder. "I'm assuming Waylen will have to use the tender to get far enough away from the boat I can safely retrieve the patient. I just hope this storm doesn't get any worse because hovering here is like trying to hold a bronco steady with a piece of string."

"I don't know. You make it look easy. And you seem to know a lot about boats and proper rescue practices. Have you done many? You mentioned something about preferring them, earlier."

And there it was. The same tension straining her shoulders. The slight hitch in her breath sounding across the comms. He'd definitely hit a nerve.

"I've done a bit of everything."

"That's not really an answer."

"It's the only one you're going to get."

"That doesn't sound suspicious, at all."

"I thought men liked an air of mystery when it came to women?"

Well damn. He couldn't fault her there.

His headset clicked.

"Blake, this is Waylen. Do you read me?"

Some of the stiffness left her muscles. "Copy that."

"Does my traitorous best friend have that basket ready, yet?"

"Ready and waiting. How's our patient?"

"Not great, but he should be okay to make the

trip up without Kian having to shimmy down or jump. As long as you can hold that bird steady."

"I didn't plow your ass into the boat when I had the chance, now, did I? You just focus on getting him secured inside that basket, and I'll worry about the gusting winds and raging waves making it impossible to hover."

"Point noted. We're doing this the hard way. I'll load him into the tender and go fifty feet from the stern. That should keep the mast out of the equation. While I'm prepping the injured, I need you to radio the puddle pirates — I mean the Coast Guard. They're apparently thirty minutes out. But the boat's taking on water. We need them sooner."

"Tell her I said to abandon—"

"Already told her, and I'll be repeating it. For now, let's deal with one situation at a time. The tender has no lights. All you'll see is a headlamp."

"I've worked with less."

Blake muttered under her breath, again. What Kian assumed was another slip, then gave him a quick glance. "Sounds like you drew the long straw this time. Of course, you haven't had to reel the guy in, yet, or treat him while getting bounced around in the back of a chopper. But if you manage not to puke by the time we reach one of the hospitals, I'll buy you a cup of coffee as a thank you."

"I'll hold you to that."

She laughed. "I can't help but notice you sound

far more excited about risking your ass dangling halfway out of a chopper trying to stabilize a spinning basket, than you did safely sitting inside circling the volcano. Which you realize is crazy, right?"

"Sweetheart, I'll take literally anything to do with water over fire, any day."

Sweetheart? Why had that slipped out?

Kian waited to see if Blake might tip the machine over in an attempt to dump him out the open door for using the endearment, but she merely laughed.

"Like I said. Crazy. Okay, hold on... This is where the fun really starts."

Blake eased the chopper back, staying far enough away the downwash didn't complicate Waylen's part of the mission, especially when just keeping the small craft upright and steady was going to be hard enough. It took a few moments before that headlight appeared on the deck, a small beacon of hope in the eerie darkness. With no power, the big sailboat was nothing more than a slightly lighter smear against the black waves.

Blake must have hit some kind of spotlight because the entire back end of the vessel illuminated a moment later. Emphasizing the nauseating roll of the deck as the boat rode each wave, looking as if it might capsize at any second.

Kian rubbed his eyes, staring at the large letters

scrolled across the back. "Am I seeing things or is that boat called *Waylen*?"

"You're not seeing things."

"Doesn't that seem odd?"

"The name or the fact your buddy shares it? Because they're both odd, to me."

Kian nodded. "Agreed. I don't suppose you know the captain?"

"Of the Waylen? She's a friend of mine. Her name's Presley. She owns Driftwood Tours."

Well damn. Talk about an act of providence.

"Now, that's interesting. I'm lowering the basket—"

He inhaled when a sharp gust sent them reeling sideways, spinning the chopper a full three-sixty before Blake wrangled the helicopter back into position. She grunted when it dropped a few feet, shaking her head as she rasped into the mic.

"We're getting some severe wind sheer with this inbound system. Hold on. It's only going to get rougher."

"If you think it's too dangerous—"

"Screw that. I've never left a crew member or friend behind, yet, and I'm not starting tonight. Endeavor to do more, rather than less, as they say. And I'll do whatever I have to, but be prepared for the basket to spin."

Kian stared at her, tapping his headset. It had cut out for a second and he'd missed half of what she'd said. Something about doing more rather than less?

No doubts about it — Blake Garrett was as mysterious as she'd claimed.

Blake must have wondered why he hadn't responded because she gave him a quick side eye, waiting for him to nod, before focusing out the window. Though, even with the spotlight beaming on the surface, it was hard to judge the distance.

How she was hovering with zero reference points and no light sources was a freaking mystery. Sure, she had instruments, but with the waves cresting a good six feet and the wind blowing in every direction, he was surprised she hadn't smashed them into the boat. Or worse... dumped them in the water.

No use worrying about how great she was with Waylen nearly in position. Instead, Kian worked the controls, holding the basket steady once it got within a few feet of the tender. His buddy reached for it, missed, then managed to grab it when Blake swung it back toward him.

The line pulled against the hoist, but Blake kept the machine steady, looking far too comfortable as she moved her hands and feet, constantly adjusting to the changing conditions.

It took Waylen a few attempts to get the patient in the proper position, before he was twirling his hand — signaling Kian to start the hoist.

Blake inched them over enough the tender wasn't still being bombarded by the rotor's downwash as the basket slowly closed in on the open door. It took a bit of finessing and a whole lot of luck to maneuver the damn thing in on his own with the winds constantly pushing the unit away, but he managed it — got the man out and positioned across the other row of seats. A thorough body sweep, and Kian had the man's shirt cut off and a small saline drip hooked up to his arm as he dealt with the open cut on his forehead.

"How is he?"

Kian sighed. "He's got second and third degree burns to his face, neck, shoulders and chest, along with a decent laceration across his temple. Damn thing's bleeding like a faucet."

"In that case, we should head for the Kona Community Hospital. While Ka'u's closer, Kona's a level three trauma center, and it sounds like he'll need the advanced care. I'll radio ahead and get clearance to land at their grass helipad. The flight shouldn't take more than about twenty minutes. Let me know if it gets too rough, and I'll see if I can find smoother air. Though, between the storm system and the volcano, I don't think there's any calm air left."

"Compared to treating wounded soldiers in the back of a Black Hawk trying to avoid gunfire and RPG's this is nice."

She chuckled, giving him a nod as he focused on his patient. Stemming the bleeding while trying to keep the damaged skin clean and clear. Getting bucked by gusting winds every minute didn't make his job any easier. But he managed to keep the guy breathing while Blake made the short journey without a hitch. It wasn't until they were on their approach to the helipad that she blew out a raspy breath.

"I swear, if my engine filters are buggered, Hawk's going to get my boot up his ass."

"Problem, Blake?"

"Nothing I can't handle. There's just a bit more ash than I'd been hoping for. But we're not in any danger."

Right, and his shirt was still white.

"Hawk did say to send him the bill."

"Like I'm going to charge the man for asking me to do the right thing." She snorted. "Short final for the helipad. Buckle up."

Skilled, beautiful, and a sense of honor. This woman was definitely the full package.

Kian took his seat, keeping his patient from rolling as Blake eased onto the ground, barely shaking the helicopter as it touched down on the hospital's helipad. She reduced the throttles, motioning to the staff waiting beyond the fence.

A brief pause, then the doors opened, a group of nurses and doctors swarming the chopper. Kian helped them put the man on a stretcher then hopped out, striding beside them as he rattled of vitals and what treatments he'd undertaken. Five minutes, and the guy was in one of the trauma rooms, a full panel of staff overseeing his care.

Kian hung around until he was sure he wouldn't be needed, anymore, before making his way outside. Smoke scented the air, the odd flake of ash swirling across the pavement.

"How's your patient?"

He glanced to his right, smiling at Blake. He'd wondered if she'd left, already, and he couldn't stop the billow of warmth through his chest that she'd waited for him. "Critical. They're putting him in a drug-induced coma until they can thoroughly assess the burns. I doubt he'll be conscious anytime soon."

"Then, I guess it's lucky you and your buddy, Waylen were nearby."

"We weren't the ones who flew a helicopter in the midst of a storm with a volcano erupting thirty miles away."

She shrugged. "It'll make for a fun story one day. Which reminds me... What did you mean when you said it was interesting that Presley was the captain of the Waylen?"

"Let's just say your friend and mine go way back."

Blake frowned, tilting her head to the side before she inhaled, a flash of color staining her cheeks.

"That's why he looked familiar. I knew I'd seen him before. He's that gangly kid in the photo with Presley at that skanky bar we always go to."

Blake huffed. "I can't believe she lied to me. That she named her boat after the guy but claimed she couldn't remember his name. She definitely owes me a beer, now."

Kian cleared his throat. "Photo? Skanky bar?"

"It's nothing important, just an old photo of them on the wall in this place we frequent."

"Sounds like your friend's keeping her past as secret as Waylen. Until tonight, I didn't even know he'd been crushing on Presley for the past twenty years."

"We don't really talk too much about our pasts. No one wants to hear about all that baggage. Better to make new memories than recount old ones."

"And that's exactly the kind of answer I'd expect from someone who's named her helicopter company *Huna*. That means secret in Hawaiian, doesn't it?"

A smile tugged at her sexy mouth. "Look who's been studying."

"Never know when there's going to be a pop quiz." He glanced at his watch. "Damn, it's pretty late, but I should see if I can get those cameras to the deputy chief."

"Already took care of that for you. We're right next to the Kona Sheriff's department. They said they'd send an officer to deliver them to the right people. I figured it'd be faster since I didn't know how long you'd be stuck here."

"That was incredibly nice of you. Thanks." He arched a brow. "So… you said if I didn't puke, you'd buy me a coffee." He waved at his shirt. "Not a speck of puke on it."

"Nope. Just blood. Which is a shame. It's a very flattering shirt."

He grinned. "Guess I'll have to get myself another one. So, coffee?"

"Where we get coffee depends on whether we're making a return run to get Waylen and Presley." She walked over to him. "Any update from them?"

"I just talked to him. He and Presley are getting a room by that marina where she had her boat towed. I said I'd meet up with him tomorrow, though, that means I'll have to rent another car. I left mine at the ranch."

"Maybe if you're nice, I'll give you a lift. Speaking of which, we should head back to Waikoloa, first. My mechanic's part vampire. He's going to give my ride a good once-over so everything should be good-to-go by morning. Unless after flying with me, you'd prefer to drive?"

"It might be safer…" He coughed when she smacked his chest. "I'd love a ride in the morning. But coffee, first."

"Then, follow me, sailor."

4

*F*ollow her?

That's exactly what Kian was afraid of because after only a couple of hours in her presence, he wanted to follow her everywhere.

Which was crazy, wasn't it? Especially when she was giving off clear signals that she wasn't the type to have a casual encounter. Not that he tried to charm every beautiful woman he met into his bed. In fact, he'd been too busy trying to find a way to fit into civilian life — jumping with his buddies from one adventure to the next just to get that adrenaline fix — that he hadn't tried to have even a one-night stand since retiring.

Not that he thought he was going to get anywhere close to a physical encounter with Blake. But he'd be lying if he didn't admit he wanted one. And he had a feeling one night wouldn't be enough.

Blake made her way back to the grass pad, motioning him to get in the front seat. He opened the door, noticing she'd moved all the boxes she'd had stacked there previously. Not that he knew if she'd simply dropped them off or if she'd purposely cleared the space so he could ride up front beside her. But he liked thinking she'd done it specifically for him.

Blake waited until he was strapped in then ran through a few checks before spooling up the engines. The chopper rocked slightly as everything sprang to life, though it did sound a bit rougher than before. He thought about asking her, but she had them lifting off and heading toward the resort before he could form all the words because watching her fly…

It was hypnotic. How she moved her hands and feet, her body swaying a bit as if she was dancing to music only she heard. The woman was stunning. And incredibly skilled.

He tapped her shoulder, motioning to the instrument panel. "I was right. This bird is loaded. How long have you been flying?"

She pursed her lips then made a point of looking out the bubble. It wasn't obvious, but he noticed the slight furrow of her brow and how the left corner of her mouth twitched. She was deciding what to tell him.

"Forever, really. It runs in the family, but I got

my official license at sixteen." She glanced over at him, a genuine smile curving her lips. "Haven't looked back, since."

Christ she was beautiful when she smiled. All pretty pink lips with a few laugh lines around her mouth. What he wouldn't give to taste it.

"I'd ask you what kind of flying you've done, but you already told me. A bit of everything, right?"

She laughed, the easy sound sending a shiver down his spine. "You've got a good memory."

"You made a point of saying it was the only answer I'd get, so it's hard to forget."

That smile fell. Just vanished as she sighed, looking straight ahead, again. "Like I said. We all have baggage, and I prefer not to dwell on that. Besides, flying's flying. Whether you're taking people on a tour, making supply runs or ferrying folks between cities and hospitals, it's essentially the same thing. Haven't you heard? We're just taxi drivers with unique rides."

"Maybe. But I doubt every pilot could have pulled off that water rescue." Kian held up his hands. "I'm not going to press for more information. Just making an observation."

"Let's just say that bit of everything included more than most pilots get."

"Building that air of mystery, I see."

That got a smile lifting her lips, again. Another deep laugh filling the cockpit. "I think we're starting to understand each other. So, I'm assuming you guys are staying at the main resort?"

"Yeah. How'd you know?"

"Hawk mentioned the place had blocked off a bunch of rooms for the sailors flying in for Gadsden's retirement party. Made an educated guess you and your buddies were part of that."

"It made arranging everything easy. And the place is much nicer than we're accustomed to."

"The perks of retirement. My helipad and hanger are just up ahead. We'll land there, and I'll give you a lift over to the resort. With Kilauea erupting and it being so late, their lounge might be the only place we can grab coffee."

"Whatever you say. I'm still following."

She snorted, shaking her head as she broadcasted some kind of radio call then made her approach. Once again, he noted how smooth she was. How efficient. No plowing it on like he'd experienced in the Teams. Just a slight pause then they were on the helipad.

It took Blake a good twenty minutes to shut everything down, get the tow cart positioned, then move her machine into the hanger where her mechanic was waiting. The guy looked local, his long black hair pulled back into a ponytail. He nodded as Blake explained her concerns, then disappeared behind the chopper, tools already clanking in the distance.

Blake ushered Kian through her hanger, past a set of stairs leading to what looked like some kind of loft, then out the front door and over to her vehicle. Another minute, and they were heading for the resort, soft music playing in the background.

He smiled when she glanced over at him. "So, you drive a Jeep."

Her face scrunched up, and damn, she looked adorable. "Is that a problem?"

"Nope. Exactly the kind of ride I'd pictured. Standard, to boot."

She stared at him as if she thought he was crazy. Maybe banged his head in the chopper, earlier. "What fun is owning a car if you're not going to actually drive it?"

"Can't argue with you there."

"I'm guessing you're a truck kind of guy."

"You get that from Hawk, too, or are you just good at guessing?"

She shrugged. "All you spec op guys are truck guys. Gotta have somewhere for all that gear."

"What gear?"

"You know, the stuff you're supposed to leave behind when you retire but somehow finds its way into your personal stash." She whistled. "I've seen Hawk's *office supply* room. It has more weapons than the sheriff's station."

Kian chuckled. "It's good to be prepared."

"For what? A small invasion?"

"Says the woman who happened to have a collapsible rescue basket and ladder stashed under the seats of her helicopter. Face it… You're not so different, you just have a unique ride, as you put it."

She laughed, and it was just as intoxicating as in the chopper. "I'm going to have to watch what I say because you're like an elephant. Have you got one of those eidetic memories or something?"

"I just like to listen. You never know when someone's going to slip in something important."

"Talk about ominous."

"You seem to remember everything I've said, too."

The smile she flashed him would have knocked him on his ass if he hadn't already been sitting down. It was sin and promise — a hint of the real Blake shining through. "That's just because you're cute."

He coughed, laughing as she parked the Jeep. "You are, without a doubt, the most unique woman I've ever met."

"Good. I'd hate to be boring."

Kian offered his hand once he'd rounded the vehicle, wondering if she'd take it or smack him up the backside of his head, instead. Blake stared at his palm for a few seconds, just like back at the Brotherhood ranch, then slipped her hand in his.

He did his best not to react, but it cost him. Took all his focus to smile, then start walking without staring at their joined hands. Commenting on how her smaller palm fit perfectly in his, the rough callouses testament that she was so much more than she appeared.

He led her over to the lounge, then inside. Not that they stayed long when everyone stopped and stared as if they'd never seen a couple holding hands, before. Though, the large splatters of blood across his shirt probably had more to do with it than anything else.

Instead, Blake ordered some coffee and muffins to go, then followed him through the resort and up to his suite. She hovered at the entrance, looking as if she was deciding on whether it was safe to venture inside before slowly crossing the threshold.

Kian worked the buttons on his shirt, all the while smiling at her. "I won't pounce. Promise."

Blake headed for the small table next to the kitchenette, placing the food and drinks on the top. "I can handle myself if you do."

"I wouldn't expect anything less. But I'm not the kind of guy who would…you know…" He let the rest go unsaid, and she merely nodded. As if she'd already taken stock of the kind of guy he was and had found him trustworthy enough to accompany to his room.

Or maybe she was a black belt in five different kinds of martial arts and wasn't at all concerned if he behaved poorly.

He wouldn't. Ever. But she didn't know that. A reminder they were essentially strangers, though he had a feeling he'd still know practically nothing about her even after spending months together. That baggage she didn't want to unpack.

More like a past she was running from. It wasn't obvious. But he prided himself in reading people — had been trained in various interrogation techniques — and Blake Garrett had the look. The way she studied every person as if she'd be tested on whether they were wearing a hat or carrying a briefcase later, while simultaneously positioning herself so no one ever got a good look at her told him everything she wouldn't. She was either hiding from a relationship gone bad, or she was running from the cops. And since she'd voluntarily gone into the sheriff's station — had been vetted enough to work for Hawk — he bet his ass it was the first.

Which seemed a bit odd since she definitely carried herself as if she could kick his ass if needed. Just like she'd said.

He mulled over the thoughts as he grabbed a new shirt, then settled on the seat next to her. She handed him his coffee, placing the muffins on top of the bag and her keys off to one side.

He accepted the cup and took a cautious sip. "I don't know what kind of coffee this is but it's always good."

"It's a local Kona brand. Definitely one of the perks of living on the Big Island."

He nodded, relaxing back in the chair. "So, this is where most people would make idle conversation. You know, like where are you from? What did you do before you moved here? That sort of stuff."

"How do you know I wasn't born here?"

"Because Waylen was born here, and there's no way he would have forgotten you. And before you say anything, no... The island isn't nearly big enough for you to have gone unnoticed."

She snorted, wiping her mouth when she obviously wondered if she'd dribbled some coffee. "Damn, you're smooth. And no, I wasn't born here. Moved over about eighteen months ago."

"New job opportunity?"

"Let's just say I needed a fresh start."

Kian nodded, sipping more of his coffee. She was good. Answering the question, but like before, not really telling him anything. Another sign she was definitely running from something. Only he was starting to think it was more than just a creepy ex. That maybe it was darker. Far more sinister because she had that look, too. Of someone who'd gone through hell and barely made it out the other side. The same one he had whenever he chanced a glance in the mirror.

"Is that when you met Presley?"

Blake smiled, her muscles noticeably relaxing.

Which made sense if Presley was part of this fresh start and not associated to whatever she'd left behind. What she obviously deemed as a safe topic. "It was shortly after I'd arrived. We were both in that skanky bar I mentioned. It's close to the marina where she docks her boats. Anyway, some asshole was giving her a hard time, so she told him to get lost and stood up to leave, when he snagged her arm."

She snorted. "Presley spun and grabbed the guy by the balls, telling him off before shoving him away. Which would have been fine if it had ended with that, but his buddy decided to get involved, and…" She shrugged. "I don't like an unfair fight."

Kian chuckled. "So you got involved."

"I'm not sure involved is the right term. It makes it sound like I tried to reason with the jerk."

"And you didn't?"

"You can't reason with guys like that."

"So, you what? Kicked his ass?"

"Like I said. I can handle myself. Anyway, we've been friends ever since."

She took a long drink of her coffee. "Enough about me. You and Waylen look like you go back a long way."

Changing the subject. She was better than good.

"It's gotta be at least fifteen years. Ever since BUD/S training. He's a giant pain in my ass, but…"

"But you'd be lost without him."

"Something like that. After all the missions, your team becomes family, which is why we're all out here."

"You guys planning on staying long?"

"That remains to be seen. Though, I have to admit, I'm loving the view."

Blake all but choked on her coffee, shaking her head as she leaned back in the chair. "Do any of your lines ever actually work?"

"Rarely."

"But you keep trying."

Kian leaned forward. "I figure there's got to be a lady out there who'll appreciate my charm."

"Let me know when you find her."

Kian placed his hand over his heart. "Ouch."

Blake grabbed one of the muffins and started eating, but he didn't miss the way her mouth kicked up, even more.

Kian picked at the food, wondering if she'd be willing to sit on the couch and watch some TV when she sighed, then pushed to her feet.

She gazed over at him when he rose beside her, looking as if she wasn't quite sure whether to push past him or lean against the wall. "It's late, and we've got an early start."

He nodded, stepping sideways so she wouldn't feel trapped. "Are you okay to drive? You look exhausted."

"Just what every girl wants to hear."

"You know what I mean. While I suspect you'd never admit it, I'm sure flying in those conditions took a toll."

"Nothing I haven't done before…"

She cringed the moment the words slipped free. Another mistake, judging by the hint of red across her cheeks. The way she pursed her lips as she closed her eyes for a moment.

"Right. One of those bits. Come on, I'll walk you to your Jeep."

"You don't need——"

"I know. And yet, I'm still going to insist." He motioned toward the door. "Just, humor me. The last thing I need is to have to bail you out of jail because you had to kick some creep's ass."

She made a show of rolling her eyes, but he didn't miss how the tension in her muscles eased. Some of that stiff bravado slipping away. She walked to the door, stopping short as she turned. "I forgot my ke——"

But he was too close — had been too fixated on the sway of her hips and how devastating she looked in those khaki shorts to stop in time, his momentum carrying him into her then up against the door.

She inhaled as her back hit the slab, her hands landing on his chest. He managed to catch his weight on one hand before he'd completely crushed her between his body and the door, giving his head a shake as he stared down at her. Fully expecting her to "handle herself".

Kian opened his mouth to explain, when her gaze dipped to his lips then up again, a raspy breath sounding between them. Her fingers twitched against his shirt, the tips brushing across his flesh.

He focused on her eyes, wondering how he'd missed the flecks of amber amidst the blue. The darker ring around the edge, not to mention a subtle sweet scent on her skin he was sure had nothing to do with perfumes or body lotions.

He lifted his other hand, smoothing his thumb along her jaw, loving how her breath caught, her pupils eclipsing some of that blue. He waited, drinking all of her in, when she pressed into his palm.

That did him in. Had him leaning forward, pausing with their breath mixing — his mouth brushing against hers. He waited to see if she'd shove him away, closing the scant distance when she relaxed against the door, his fingers tightening around his shirt.

Blake didn't even hesitate, tugging him closer, a low moan sounding between them as he slipped his hand behind her head — deepened the kiss.

Talk about paradise.

But this had nothing to do with the palm trees or the warm ocean breezes. This was all Blake. The taste of her mouth, the feel of her body snugged against his. He let her catch her breath, kissing his way down her neck then back, capturing her mouth, again.

How was this kiss even better? Hotter? Far more intense as if someone had cranked up the heat. Had him gasping for air once he'd finally moved back.

Had she whispered his name? Looking as if she was going to tackle them both to the ground. That pouncing he'd joked about earlier. Until a car back-fired somewhere outside, the loud pop echoing through the open window.

Blake jumped, her gaze flying to the window as the sensuous atmosphere shattered. Went from searing heat to icy cold in the space of a heartbeat. Kian cursed under his breath, stepping back when her muscles tensed, her gaze scanning the room as if she'd expected to find someone else standing there.

He looked over his shoulder, too, wondering if he'd missed something, but the room was empty. Just the curtains fluttering in the breeze.

Screwed. No other way to put it. Not with how she was staring at him. Eyes wide. Her weight shifted to her toes as if she was gearing up for a fight.

"Blake I…"

He didn't know what to say because he wasn't sorry for kissing her. Instead, he grabbed her keys off the table. The reason he was in this mess.

It took her a second to snap back — focus on his outstretched hand.

She closed her eyes for a moment, then took the keys, fisting her hand around them before she nodded. Managed to reach behind her back and open the door. "Thanks."

"I'd say I'm sorry but…"

She snorted. "Pretty sure I was all-in, too. And it's not that I'm not interested or that I don't want to…" She huffed out a breath. "It's…"

"Complicated?"

"Cliché, but true." She backed up through the door, still staring at him.

"I should still walk you to your Jeep."

"Trust me. No one's going to mess with me, and I… I could use some air."

"It feels wrong, and my mother raised me better than that."

"How about a compromise, and you watch out the window? The lot where I parked is directly below."

"Not really a compromise, but…" He sighed, aware he wouldn't win this argument, and the last thing he wanted to do was send her running for the hills.

Kian stuffed his hands in his pockets so he didn't try to reach out — tug her against him. "For the record, not every guy's looking for easy. Some of us don't mind having to find our way through a maze, first."

She stopped, tilting her head to one side. "And when you discover there're monsters hiding on the path? Then, what?"

"I slay them."

Blake shook her head. "You're…"

"Charming? Irresistible?" He gave her a smile, hoping he edged the odds in his favor as he eased some of the tension. "The man of your dreams?"

"Unexpected." She glanced away for a moment, but not before he saw the smile lifting her lips. "If you still want a lift over to that hotel, I'll be in the parking lot at seven sharp."

"I'll be there."

She nodded. "It'll take us about thirty minutes. If you're lucky, we should arrive in time for you to still be a cockblock for your buddy Waylen."

Kian stared at her, wishing he knew what the hell to say to ease the shadowed look in her eyes. "I realize they have history, but Waylen's not that charming."

Blake scoffed. "Please, she named her boat *and* a cat after the guy. He doesn't need to be charming."

She took a few steps into the corridor. "Seven sharp, sailor, or I'm leaving without you."

Kian stared at the door once she'd closed it, her footsteps fading down the hallway. Talk about being an ass…

He never should have kissed her. Sure, she'd returned the kiss — had been right there with him. Chest heaving. Pulse tapping triple time under her skin. All-in as she'd phrased it. But he knew fear when he saw it, and Blake had been terrified.

Not of him. At least, not in the sense that she thought he'd hurt her. More the fact he'd gotten close. Dodged some of her defenses.

He moved over to the window, following her as she exited the building then darted into the parking lot — ready to vault off the balcony and shimmy down the side of the building if anyone so much as looked at her the wrong way. He could only see a glimpse of her as she got into her Jeep, but he saw it pull away, the taillights fading around a corner.

This definitely wasn't how he'd wanted the night to end. But it had made one thing clear. Whether it was fate or just really weird timing, he was already falling for the girl. And he had absolutely no idea what to do about it.

*B*lake stood next to her helicopter, wondering how she'd gone from hiding in the shadows, to stepping into the light in such a short time. Had it really only been three weeks since Kilauea had started erupting and everything had changed?

Since Kian had walked into her life.

Because it felt longer. A lifetime, ago.

Though, maybe that was because she hadn't really been living before that night. Had been going through the motions, trudging through each day just trying to survive. Staying on the fringes. Anything to avoid being noticed.

Noticed meant she might be recognized or inadvertently get her photo taken. Something that could make its way back to the Russo family — blow her cover. And for the past eighteen months, she'd had no trouble keeping to herself. Other than her outings with Presley, Blake had been a virtual recluse. She only flew jobs that had been secured with clients the Marshal Service had set up for her, Hawk's organization being one of them. She also helped out the various police stations, and the ranger units. The kind of people who'd been deemed low risk.

So, accompanying Kian damn near every night to what had become his team's local bar was dangerous. Borderline suicidal because it meant she was out there, setting herself up for one hell of a possible backlash.

She groaned. As usual, she was being overly paranoid. She was still following the rules the Marshals had drilled into her. Still taking every precaution possible. After all, wasn't she supposed to be able to live, too? Have some semblance of happiness after all she'd given up?

She wasn't sure, but she'd be damned if she could stop. Step back into those shadows because for the first time in her life, she'd found someone she wasn't sure she could walk away from.

Which was crazy in its own right. Sure, Kian had given her clear signals he wanted more than just a casual fling while he and his buddies were helping out. In fact, they were already talking about staying. About joining Hawk's outfit — something about buying that stupid bar because the owners had decided it was time to move on. Nothing concrete, yet, but the possibility was there. And that's what was slowly chipping away at her resolve to stay distant.

She glanced at Kian when he laughed. Since their accidental first kiss, he'd been playing it cool. Allowing her to decide when they got physical. Which had been pretty much every time she'd been close to him. They'd kept it on the down low. Had managed to avoid any kind of public display that would broadcast they were more than just buddies who hung out. What she assumed his friends still thought. And while she hadn't quite made it into Kian's bed, it was headed that way. And she knew, once they crossed that line, there would be no coming back. That he'd hold the only part of her she'd salvaged from her past.

She gazed at the ground, toeing the concrete as she warred with the voices arguing in her head. It wasn't just the risk that was eating at her. It was the lying. True, it was necessary — the one rule she couldn't break for any reason — but it still felt wrong. Especially when simply being close to him — to Presley and Waylen and the rest of Kian's crew — put them in danger, and she hated keeping that from them. They'd more than proven they could be trusted — probably knew more top secret intel from their years in Special Forces than what the Marshal Service dealt with in a year. She owed it to them to tell them the everything — allow them to decide if she was worth the possible fallout.

Or if they'd rather she disappear.

Though, neither Presley, nor Kian seemed like the kind of people who would balk at danger. In fact, none of Kian's crew seemed the type. Instead, she had a nagging suspicion they'd rally around her — use all that SEAL training to either keep her safe or take the fight to Russo.

Not an option, and it was the one thing holding her back from pouncing on Kian. What if she jumped and it turned into something serious? Permanent? Because it felt that way.

Like fate.

And she wasn't sure if she could live the rest of her life keeping that secret. Not that he wouldn't figure it out sooner or later. Kian was shrewd. He already suspected she was running. Or maybe hiding. *Something* that kept her from posing for a selfie or allowing the local newspaper to mention her in a story they'd just wrapped up on Presley and Waylen. Hometown couple reuniting after facing death together. Some *feel-good* piece that was sure to put Driftwood Tours on the map.

Not just the journalist had been puzzled when Blake had refused. Kian's team had been, too. All of them unsure why she'd passed up an opportunity that would have resulted in more work. Thankfully, they'd let it slide. But she knew Kian was working through all the possible scenarios, and it wouldn't take him long to land on the only one that made sense.

A damn Catch-22.

Blake looked up, smiling when Kian glanced over at her, that boyish charm making it seem ten degrees hotter. He turned and said something to Waylen — probably razzing the guy because Waylen and Presley had just discovered their lack of restraint, and condoms, had resulted in her getting pregnant — then started toward her, his sexy swagger nearly taking her to her knees.

God he was gorgeous. And she knew she wouldn't be able to hold out, much longer.

He stopped far closer than a friend would, leaning in until his mouth was level with hers. Those sexy lips within kissing distance. "Something on your mind, sweetheart?"

He'd been calling her that for over a week. Maybe longer because she didn't even remember when it had started. As if he'd snuck it in without her noticing and by the time she'd finally grasped the full weight of the endearment, it had been too late to call foul.

Especially when she loved the way it rolled off his tongue.

Blake held her ground, knowing he enjoyed it when she challenged him. "Maybe you should tell me."

"That sounds dangerous."

"Maybe what's on my mind is dangerous."

He arched a brow. "I don't know. I've been walking this maze for a few weeks, now, and I'm still waiting for all those monsters to show up."

She did her best not to react, realizing she'd failed when his mouth twitched a bit. His only tell. "Trust me. They're real."

"So's my promise to slay them."

God, he was serious. Serious and brave and she wanted him to slay them. Give her a moment's peace without constantly watching over her shoulder.

Kian frowned. "Hey… Are you okay? You look pale, all of a sudden."

"I…"

She gave him a nudge when Waylen and Presley headed their way, eyes wide. Mouths pursed.

Kian muttered a curse under his breath, taking her hand as he turned. "You've already got your girl. Must you interrupt my attempts to charm Blake?"

Waylen snorted, though, it sounded forced. "If it hasn't happened after all this time, brother…"

"Wise ass. So, where's the fire? Because you both look like you just lost your best friend." He inhaled. "Shit, is everything okay with the baby? I mean, it's insanely early, but do you need medical help? A trip to emergency? I've got my bag—"

KRIS NORRIS

"Whoa, buddy, breathe. Christ, for someone who never loses their cool, you just hit DEFCON one without any reason. We're fine, and as far as I know, the baby's fine. Like you said. It's early, but other than some puking, it's good."

Kian slapped Waylen on the chest. "Don't freaking scare me like that. Dealing with tangos and gunshot wounds is one thing. Thinking Presley might be hurt…"

Presley hitched out a hip. "I'm standing right here. And I'm fine. But…"

"But…"

She sighed, focusing on Blake. "It's about that newspaper article they just wrote."

Blake nodded, the inklings of fear slithering down her spine. "What about it?"

Blake had already scoured every word, every image, to ensure the newspaper crew hadn't taken photos of her behind her back. Maybe mentioned her name. Not that the Russo family would recognize Garrett, but if there was even a hint of something familiar, they'd make the connection and come looking.

Presley pursed her lips even more, glancing at Waylen and Blake knew that everything was about to get ugly. "Remember Mano? That detective we had looking into my scumbag ex? He just called. Wanted to know if we'd seen the follow-up video, yet."

Blake swallowed, coughed when it didn't get past the lump in her throat before trying, again. Nearly choking, this time. "Follow-up video? What video?"

Presley held out her phone. "I... I don't know what to say. I mean... I had no idea. And..."

But Blake already had the damn thing running. Staring as some twenty-year old kid started talking. Commenting on the article then claiming how the newspaper had neglected to include the best part. How it had all started with a harrowing rescue at sea.

It only got worse from there. Live footage of her hovering over the ocean, Kian half hanging out of the chopper as Waylen tried to heave the injured man into the basket. Snapshots of the machine dancing in the gusting wind, everything backlit by the crimson glow of the volcano. The only saving grace because it kept the helicopter silhouetted in the sky. Nothing but a black outline against the red. What might make this catastrophe nothing more than a nuisance.

Until it faded into a photo of her leaning against the hospital wall as she'd waited for Kian to come back out. It was dark and slightly out-of-focus, but there was no doubt it was her. Not to anyone who knew her.

Having the guy end by saying that while he wouldn't divulge her name, she was certainly living up to her nearly Five-O namesake, was the last deadly straw. The one that would have her handler, U.S. Deputy Marshal Adam Porter, ringing her cell any moment, now.

Or worse, Henry Russo's hitmen storming the ranch.

Blake let her hand fall to her side, that photo still visible even after she closed her eyes. After everything she'd been through — all the precautions she'd taken, the years she'd stayed in the dark just to uphold her oath — she couldn't believe it would end like this.

That she'd lose everything. Again.

Fingers snapped in front of her face, and she looked up, staring into Kian's blue eyes. God, was this the last time she'd see them? See him? Feel at all safe because she realized that, now. The reason she'd gone out to the bar — spent all her free time with him. He'd already slayed half those monsters with nothing more than his smile. His strong arms around her waist.

And now, she'd have to leave.

Kian grabbed her shoulders, easing her back until her ass was braced against the chopper and he was able to shove her head down by her knees. He moved in beside her, bridging her weight as he bent over until he was level with her. Had his mouth next to her ear.

"Breathe, Blake. Try to get your lungs working or you're gonna pass out on me."

Breathe? How could she breathe when her life was crumbling around her? Only this time, she wouldn't have any hope left because he wouldn't be coming with her.

He shook his head, getting even closer. "Whatever this is, we'll deal with it. Just please... relax enough to take a breath."

Dots started eating away the edges of her vision, sliding left and right until she managed to gasp in a quick breath — stop herself from falling on the cement.

Kian lifted her up then snugged her against his chest, drawing gentle circles along her back. "That's it. In and out. Slower. Good, now hold it..."

He smiled against her forehead, dropping a soft kiss on her skin before tilting her head up. "Better. Just keep breathing."

She nodded, knowing she didn't really have any other choice. That she needed to pull herself together and take stock.

She leaned against him for a couple more minutes then eased back. Doing her best to regain her composure. Kian loosened his grip, but he didn't move away, staying close enough he'd catch her if she fainted.

Presley blinked back tears when Blake finally managed to do more than suck air in then push it out, biting at her lower lip. "God, Blake. I'm so sorry. If I'd known one of the passengers had filmed it with their phone…"

Blake managed to hold her chin high — meet Presley's expectant gaze. "It's not your fault. It's just…"

How could she tell them how epically bad this was and not tell them who she really was? What deadly consequences that five-minute video and photo might have? And not just on her. No one was safe as long as she was close.

Waylen stepped forward, slipping the phone out of her hand. "I'm assuming this is bad. Having that photo of you on the internet."

He hadn't really asked, and she could only nod, again. He looked at Kian, then back to her. "What level of bad are we talking… Kinda? Sorta? Seriously?"

When she simply stared at all of them, Waylen grunted.

He made direct eye contact. "So, it's worse than seriously."

She swallowed, hoping she wouldn't start screaming the moment she opened her mouth. "How long…" She waved at the phone, thankful she'd gotten those two words out without puking.

Waylen did something with the phone, then met her gaze. "Nearly forty-eight hours."

"Shit."

"I realize that must seem bad, but this kid's a nobody. I tell you what. I'm going to borrow the Brotherhood Protector's computers and hack my way into this asshole's account and delete the video. Then, I'll insert a virus so when he tries to get it back online, it takes his entire profile down. I'll also scan the web to see if it's been rebroadcast on any other channels. Okay?"

She stared at him, still trying to process the fact her blurry photo had been online for nearly two days, and she'd missed it, when his words caught up. "Wait. You can do that? Erase it?"

Waylen grinned. "Hell, yeah. Stay here. I'll be back." He took off with Presley, heading for Hawk's office.

Kian moved in behind her, placing his hands on her waist as if he knew she was about to bolt. Or faint. "Will that help?"

She shrugged. "It can't hurt."

"But, even if Waylen erases it, you'll be worried, won't you?"

She turned in his embrace, palming his chin. Doing her best to memorize every nuance of him, from the fine lines around his eyes to the shadowed scruff on his jaw. "Honestly, I don't know. Why don't we wait until we see what Waylen has to say?"

Kian narrowed his eyes. "Why doesn't that sound reassuring?"

"Because I'm not the only one who's paranoid?"

She worked up a smile, trying to rationalize the situation. And now that the sheer shock of seeing the video had passed, she was able to think more clearly. And maybe they were right? Maybe it hadn't gotten more than a handful of views? And what were the chances anyone connected to the Russo cartel had seen it? It's not like it had her name attached. Even the Garrett suggestion wasn't something they'd pick up on. So, chances were, she'd be fine as long as Waylen worked a miracle.

In fact, the more she ran it over in her head, the more it made sense that unless U.S. Deputy Marshal Porter called her — told her she'd blown her cover — it likely hadn't reached anyone off the island, let alone the east coast.

After all, Blake had alerts set up if anything remotely close to her or the case cropped up. And seeing as she hadn't gotten a single notification...

She took a soothing breath, hoping it had just been that paranoia getting the better of her when something glinted near the bushes.

That's all she needed before she had Kian by the waist — was tackling him to the ground. No hesitation, just a lunge and they were on the helipad, his body beneath hers, her gaze sweeping the landscape. What was probably some hitman or mafia lackey hiding in the brush ready to take them out with a sniper rifle. Or maybe a drone. Either way, she wasn't moving until she'd been proven wrong, or she was dead.

6

_B_lake crouched over Kian, keeping him pinned beneath her as she scanned the area, fully expecting a group of mafia thugs to come rushing out the bushes, guns blazing. Maybe a few grenades going off.

Kian glanced over his shoulders, obviously wondering what she was searching for. But even after thirty seconds of scouring every inch of the underbrush, there was nothing but leaves and branches swaying in the breeze. A few flowers bobbing against a light gust.

Great. Now he was really going to think she was crazy. Maybe suggest she seek professional help. That, or he was going to corner her — demand answers.

Which he deserved. She only wished she could tell him the truth. Confide in someone. Lessen the burden she'd been carrying for years. First, while under the care of the Marshal Service, then the past eighteen months, here. Alone.

Kian patted her thigh, staring up at her when she finally gazed down. And damn, he looked completely at ease. As if women bowled him over all the time. And maybe they did.

Or maybe he was simply one of the last true warriors. The kind who kept their cool, even when she was losing hers.

Kian waited until she made eye contact, giving her a slight tilt of his brow. "If you wanted to go for a tumble, sweetheart, all you had to do was say the word, and I would have taken us back to my room."

She snorted, clearing the area one more time before climbing off to one side. She knew what he was doing. How he was using humor to ease some of the tension before he'd go in for the kill. Corner her, just like she'd been thinking.

She shook her head, still unsure if the coast was clear or if she really had seen someone holding a gun. "Ass."

"Wasn't me who flipped out over some swaying branches."

"It wasn't the branches. I thought I saw…"

He waited, nudging her when she simply sat there, still staring at the brush. "Thought you saw…"

"Forget it. It must have been my imagination. A shadow or something. Did I hurt you?"

"Please. My buddies hit harder than that playing football."

"Right."

He accepted the hand she offered, rising smoothly to his feet, only he didn't stop there.

Two seconds, and he had her pinned to the side of the chopper, one arm braced against the fuselage next to her head, the other resting on her hip. Just like in his hotel room that first night. When she'd kissed him as if she'd never been that close to a man before. And hell, maybe she hadn't. Not like this, where she couldn't separate her heart from what was screaming in head.

Kian narrowed his eyes, looking as if he was still trying his best to puzzle her out before lifting his hand and tracing his fingers along her jaw. "Blake—"

"Why are you such a hard habit to break?"

He leaned in. "So, I'm a Chicago song?"

"Again, you're an ass. But corny or not, it's true. And I should know. I've had to make some difficult choices — walk away from people I cared about. Yet standing here, nothing seems as clear-cut as it used to. Just thinking about leaving…"

"Leaving?" Some of the color drained from his face as his smile fell flat. "Why would you be thinking about leaving?"

"That's not the point. What I'm saying is…" She tiptoed up — nipped at his lower lip. She didn't want to talk. Didn't want to think about how the next few hours would play out. If she really was overreacting or this was the start of the end. The fact she was blurting out every random thought as it popped into her head wasn't helping.

She palmed his face. "Shut up and kiss me."

"I'll kiss you after we talk. I can't—"

"Kian. For the next five minutes can you just pretend I didn't freak out? That everything's normal? Please?"

She didn't wait for him to answer, simply leaned forward — claimed his mouth.

How was kissing him even better than she remembered? Sweeter than the ones they'd shared last night when she'd dropped him off at the resort, again? Where they'd spent forty-five minutes saying goodbye in her Jeep?

That's when it hit her. How in the space of only a few weeks, this island had turned from a refuge into a home.

And it was all because of him.

Blake raised her hand and ran her fingers along his neck then into his hair, fisting the soft strands as he deepened the kiss. He didn't seem to care they were standing at the edge of the lawn, that his friends might be staring at them, wondering if they'd both lost their minds, he simply eased back long enough to catch a breath before kissing her, again. Harder. Dragging her body against his, the firm ridge pressing against her hip proof he was completely focused on her.

Footsteps sounded behind them followed by a chuckle. "Christ, we can't leave you two alone for five minutes before you're necking like teenagers."

Kian flipped Waylen off without breaking contact, giving her one last kiss before shaking his head and inching back. But he stayed close, as if he expected her to run off if he wasn't physically touching her. And any other time, she would have. Would have turned on her heels, climbed into her chopper and left. Back to her hanger where she would have packed up her meager belongings and caught the first flight out.

Except where she wasn't sure she could, this time.

Kian pulled her a bit closer, turning to face Waylen and Presley. "Well?"

Waylen shook his head in mock disappointment. "I can't believe you had any doubts I'd get the video taken down."

"I wasn't doubting you. I was simply wondering if you could stop kissing Presley long enough to get the job done. Talk about two people acting like teenagers."

"Wasn't us making out against the chopper a minute ago."

Kian's lips quirked. "So, it's gone?"

Waylen snorted. "Nice deflection. And yeah, it's gone. I did a search to see if the guy had uploaded it to any other sites but came up empty. Not that I can guarantee it's not still out there, but if I couldn't find it…"

"Then, no one can. Got it." Kian nudged her. "What level are we at, now?"

She feigned a small smile, nodding at Waylen. "Undetermined. Could you tell how many views it had?"

Waylen glanced at Kian then back to her. "It said a few thousand, which really isn't that many. However…"

Was she frozen, again? Because it felt that way. That one word reigniting all the panic she'd barely gotten under control.

She managed to swallow most of it — get her tongue working, again. "However? That sounds bad."

"Not bad. But I want to be completely honest. And the truth is, I have no way of knowing how often they update those statistics. If it's live, hourly or just once a day."

"I see. So, it could be more than just a few thousand views."

"Possibly. But… even if it was ten thousand, it's still relatively small. Nothing close to going viral."

"Right." She reached over and gave his hand a

squeeze. "Regardless. Thank you. I can't believe you did that for me."

Waylen scrunched up his face. "Why wouldn't I? Anything for my girl's best friend."

Blake nodded, trying to be optimistic when the full weight of his words sunk in. That's when she realized she'd have to leave Presley behind, too. And Waylen and Lane and Cassie and the rest of Kian's crew. The people she'd come to see as friends, despite having just met them because that's how they made her feel. Like she was family.

Tears pooled in her eyes, and she had to fight hard to blink them away. Pretend a spec of dust had blown into one of them when a few drops slipped out. Not that Kian believed her. She'd barely managed to wipe her cheeks before he was leaning over her, mouth pursed. Brow furrowed.

"Okay, enough is enough. It's time we had that talk because you're really starting to scare me."

He moved closer, glancing at Waylen and Presley over his shoulder as he lowered his head. "I know you're running from something. That much has been obvious from the start. But I can't fix anything if I don't know what's wrong."

Fix it? How could she tell him that the only way he could fix anything was if he had a time machine and she could go back — unsee everything. Or better... Stop Russo before there had been anything for her *to* see. "While I love the sentiment, this isn't something you can fix."

"So, I'm right, and there is something."

"Kian."

"How do you know I can't fix it when you haven't even let me try? Whatever this is — whether it's trouble with the law or someone else — I can help you. It's what I do — what my team does. All you have to do is tell me what's got you so damn spooked."

He was serious. Standing there, staring into his eyes, Blake knew he wasn't joking. That if she told him the freaking Russo crime family was hunting her and that stupid video meant hired mercenaries might be closing in on her, right now, he'd simply nod and act as if it was another regular afternoon. Rally his crew and have her surrounded by armed ex-SEALs before she could blink.

But the crazier part was that she wanted to tell him. Have him tell her it was all going to be okay, even if it was a lie.

Instead, she gave him a genuine smile. "I'm sure it's fine now that Waylen took down the video. Really. I just hate having my privacy trampled on."

"You're lying." He sighed. "Not about the privacy thing. That's true. But your mouth twitches a bit whenever you're trying to brush something off, so I don't ask more probing questions. I should know. You've been doing that ever since I met you, and I'm not ashamed to admit I've been so damn focused on you, I couldn't have missed it if I'd tried. So, I'll ask, again. What's really going on?"

"Kian, I—"

"Is this a private party or can anyone bust in?"

Blake jumped, nearly socking Kian in the eye as Hawk's voice sounded behind them. It wasn't like her to not notice someone approaching, but it was the second time people had walked up on them and she'd been too engrossed in Kian to realize.

Kian closed his eyes for a moment, obviously unhappy about the intrusion, before he plastered on a smile and turned. "There's always room for you, Hawk. What's up?"

Hawk must have noticed he'd interrupted an important conversation because he stopped, glancing between them before shoving his hands in his pockets. Though, the tears drying on her cheeks probably didn't help.

Hawk gave her a once-over, his gaze still clearly assessing her as he motioned toward the machine. "I just got a call from the clinic over in Ka'u. They haven't been able to get all the supplies they need and with Kilauea still spewing ash and smoke, they've got more patients than usual. I've got one of my guys bringing back a truckload, but it'll take him hours to drive over and some of their patients just can't wait that long. I was hoping you and Blake might do me a solid and fly it out. They mentioned they could use a bit of triage help, too, and with you being a trained combat medic…"

Kian nodded. "Always happy to lend a hand, but I can't speak for Blake."

Hawk focused on her. "Well, Blake? Have you got a couple of hours free?"

She paused to glance around the area — see if there were any armed hitman biding their time behind bushes or outbuildings, but nothing suggested she'd actually spotted someone earlier. More likely it was her paranoia getting the better of her. Still… she should say no. Hop in her chopper and get as far away as possible before they all became collateral damage, just like her friends back east. The ones who'd ended up in the hospital when her boss and the district attorney had thought she'd be safe surrounded by her crew. That the Russos wouldn't chance another encounter with her division after the fallout from their first attempt.

They'd been wrong and those injuries were on her.

Blake opened her mouth to decline — make up some kind of viable excuse — buy herself enough time to bug out without them deducing her plan. Maybe trying to stop her.

Hearing herself say yes caught her by surprise. Had her inhaling because it was crazy.

Some of the patients can't wait that long.

That's what had swayed her. That if she was going to lose everything, again, the least she could do was honor her oath one last time. Even if she was the only one who knew why.

And if she got one final evening with the man she was pretty sure she'd fallen in love with, then maybe she'd be able to do the right thing.

Hawk grinned. "Excellent." He turned when a truck pulled onto the long road into the ranch. "That's your supplies, now. I'll let the clinic know you'll be there shortly. And thanks. I might have to officially put you on the docket if I keep monopolizing your services like this."

Just what she needed. More guilt for when she finally had to leave. She glanced at her cell, double checking she hadn't missed any calls. That Porter had already tried to reach her, and she'd somehow ignored the endless vibrations because she wasn't quite ready to face reality.

Maybe she really was crazy? Because Porter would have blown up her cell if he'd spotted the video, wouldn't he? If his checks and alerts had picked up on it when hers hadn't. Even with the video down, he wouldn't chance not contacting her if the damn thing had popped up on his radar. Not with Russo staging an appeal.

Kian knocked her shoulder, giving her a hard stare once she met his gaze. "Just because we have a job to do doesn't mean this discussion's over. I'll help load the supplies but consider yourself put on notice."

Oh, she was on notice, all right. It just wasn't the one he thought.

7

*L*ucky. Not that Kian really felt that way, but he had to admit. If Hawk hadn't asked Blake to fly the supplies out to the clinic, she might have bolted. Hopped into her helicopter and disappeared.

He knew it.

Sensed it.

Whether it was the haunted look in her eyes or the way she'd been checking her phone every five minutes since leaving the ranch, Kian wasn't sure. Only that if he didn't figure out how to get her to confide in him — trust that he could handle whatever had her running scared — he'd lose her.

And maybe not just from his life.

If her reaction to the photograph and video were any indication of the kind of trouble shadowing her, he could only assume her life was on the line.

Organized crime.

That had to be what she was running from. Whether it was a genetic association, a previous love connection or someone she'd crossed, it was the only threat that seemed to tick all the boxes.

Blake had tried to brush the whole thing off as shock. Kept insisting she was fine now that the images were gone. But Kian knew her better than that. Even with her keeping her past vague, he'd gotten around enough of her defenses he had a genuine idea of her personality. And Blake Garrett wasn't the kind of woman to run from a fight. Not with how she'd handled herself that first night. Or any of the rescues, since. She was steadfast. Tough. And oozed honor as much as his team did.

Which meant, she wasn't afraid for herself.

She was worried her newfound friends would suffer some sort of collateral damage.

That *he'd* get hurt.

Which seemed almost comical after all he'd faced in the Teams. The missions that never quite went as planned. The endless near-misses he and his buddies had dodged.

That fate had brought him through so he could be the force standing between her and whoever was hunting her. And it was time she realized that.

Kian straightened, smiling at one of the nurses

when she thanked him for helping. They'd arrived at the clinic three hours ago, and he'd been immersed in endless assessments since.

Which was why he'd insisted Lane accompany them. Blake hadn't been happy, mumbling something about weight and space, but Kian had simply crossed his arms and dared her challenge him.

She'd relented, mostly because she'd been bluffing. But all that really mattered in the end was that Kian had backup. Had asked Lane to do continuous perimeter checks while Kian had been busy helping out. Not only to ensure a group of tangos didn't somehow slip past him while he was focused on stopping a guy from bleeding out, but to ensure Blake didn't ditch him.

Which was definitely a possibility. All she had to do was wait until he was concentrating on a patient, before slipping back to her chopper and taking off. Even with the noise and the short amount of time it would have taken her to ready the machine, Kian doubted he could have stopped her. Not alone.

Blake obviously knew he hadn't brought his buddy along for companionship, and she'd been brooding ever since. Not always in his sight line, but he'd been able to suss her out whenever he'd gotten a tingling down his spine. That scratching between his shoulder blades that warned him everything was about to go sideways.

Like now, packing up his medic bag, half a

dozen people blocking his view of Blake. He zipped it shut without worrying if everything was in the usual place, stepping around the small crowd as he scanned the room. She'd been standing by the vending machines for the past half hour, so finding them empty turned that inkling into more of an omen.

He rolled his shoulders, reminding himself he would have heard the chopper taking off. And there was no way she would have left it behind. Not when he suspected it was one of the few tangible links to whatever secrets she was hiding.

Her one constant in what he could only imagine had been a tumultuous past.

He walked down the hallway, spotting her leaning against a pillar near the back of the room. One of the emergency exits within sprinting distance.

She barely gave him a passing glance before continuing to scan the crowd, though, what or who she was looking for, was a mystery.

Blake clenched her jaw when he moved in close. Not as close as before this whole shit show had started back at the helicopter. When she'd teased him about having something dangerous on her mind. And she'd been right. Too bad it had morphed from what he suspected was them finally tumbling around on his bed to her catching the next flight off the island.

The slip she'd made earlier. About how thinking about leaving was gutting her. But he knew she'd walk away if she was convinced it was the only way to keep everyone else safe.

A disgruntled huff, then she was meeting his gaze. Giving him some kind of stink eye. "You ready to go?"

He shuffled until he was leaning on the side of the same pillar, trying to read if she really was pissed or if she was putting on a show. Hoping they'd get into a fight, so he'd let her storm off.

Not a chance.

He motioned toward the nursing station. "They seem to have it under control, now. I'll call Lane—"

"No need." She turned until she was staring him directly in the eyes. "He's on his, what… two hundredth perimeter check. He should be back within the next five minutes. And he always makes sure he has a visual on me before he heads out for the next one. You know… in case I try to sneak out the back while you're busy. The reason you brought backup on a medical run."

She was definitely pissed, though, it didn't hide the fact she was scared, too. Terrified judging on how pale she was. The increased flutter of her pulse.

Kian took a breath, reminding himself to stay calm. Speak softly. "I didn't bring Lane solely to stop you from ditching me."

"But you thought I would, right? Because I obviously have no sense of honor."

"This has nothing to do with honor and everything to do with the fact that you've been practically crawling out of your skin since you saw that video. Look at you. It's only been four hours since Presley shared that link, and you look exhausted. The circles under your eyes, the ever-present tension in your muscles. You're primed for a fight. You think I haven't noticed how you've changed your position with every passing hour? That you went from attentive to concerned to stake-out level? Like now. You've claimed the one location that gives you a perfect view of anyone entering or leaving the facility but provides a decent amount of cover. The same spot I'd pick if I was waiting for a group of tangos to ambush the place."

Kian shifted on his feet, trying to pull himself back, but now that they were actually talking, he couldn't seem to reel it all in, again. "You'd lost that, by the way. The haunted look in your eyes you've had since we met. The guarded glances you give everyone. Sticking to the shadows. Over the past few weeks, you'd actually started to relax."

She snorted, inching closer. "I think the phrase you're looking for is that I got complacent. Careless, even."

"Or maybe you knew you were safe. That if anyone came gunning for you, they'd have to go through me, too." He paused to tuck a few loose strands of hair behind her ear. "We make one hell of a team, sweetheart. And your subconscious knows it."

He took a breath, wondering where all that calmness had gone. The easy voice he'd reminded himself to use. "So, yeah. I was slightly concerned you'd fly off and try to face this on your own. But I mostly brought Lane along because as good as I am, even I can't watch my own six. And I have absolutely no idea what kind of men might walk through that door."

Blake stared at him, mouth slightly open, eyes wide. She glanced at the entrance, her breath coming in short, sharp spurts before she closed her eyes. Let her shoulders droop as her head fell back, turning to brace her weight on the post. "No one good."

He froze. Fucking froze because of all the replies he thought he'd get, some semblance of the truth wasn't one of them.

Kian moved in front of her, taking her hands in his. "Blake. Please, talk to me."

Tears pooled in her eyes, her chin quivering as she glanced at the door, then back to him. "Don't you think I would if I could? But I can't."

"Why? I'm not afraid of whoever's chasing you—"

"Then, you're beyond crazy because you should

be." She untangled her hands from his, then took a step away. "These people don't fight fair, Kian. They don't care about collateral damage — if they end up at the top of every agency's most wanted list." She pointed at the main lobby. "They'd rather send a freaking RPG through the hospital window than let me get away. Those are the kind of men who are going to walk through that door."

"Then, we'll keep you someplace safe until we get a handle on this. Deal with it."

"Deal with it? I've spent the past three years *dealing* with it. I've watched good people nearly die because they thought they could deal with it, too."

She shook her head, her hair bouncing wildly about her shoulders as it released from the clip. "This isn't a war you can win because it doesn't matter how many you eliminate, there's always more. They have endless resources. And they'll never stop hunting me. Ever. Not as long as he's alive."

Kian reclaimed his position, taking her hands in his, again. "As long as who's alive? Who's hunting you?"

That simple question seemed to snap her back and she inhaled, as if just realizing what she'd said. How much she'd let slip.

She tugged against his hold, huffing when he refused to let go. "It doesn't matter. Christ, I've told you too much already."

She tried, again, cursing this time. "Damn it, Kian, we need to go. There're too many people. It's not safe. I never should have said yes..."

Her eyes widened a moment before she wrapped her hands around his wrists and yanked him behind the post. Shoving him off to her right as she made herself as small as possible, her gaze fixed on the door.

Kian moved in closer, waiting until a nurse walked in front of them, heading for one of the back rooms, before chancing a quick peek. Three men stood off to the side of the entrance, their button-up shirts, pale skin, and long pants clear indicators they hadn't been on the island long. But it was more the way they studied the room, pausing on every face as if searching for someone. They didn't even try to hide it, grabbing the odd person in order to get a better look.

He slipped his medic bag off his shoulder, undoing it enough to slide his hand inside — retrieve the gun he kept hidden in a pouch for emergency purposes. And based on how the men were working their way through the crowd, this was shaping up to be one hell of an emergency.

Blake tapped his thigh, shaking her head before pointing to the exit. A logical plan except where they'd be out in the open for a few seconds before clearing the door. Not to mention he had no idea if there was any cover beyond the exit.

He should have done his own perimeter checks, instead of relying on Lane. Not that he didn't trust the man, Kian just hated not knowing which strategy would garner him the best results. If they should dart across the room, or try to blend in so they could head out the front.

Whatever they chose, they needed to act quickly, before those assholes decided for them.

Having someone start screaming because they'd noticed one of the men carrying a gun was just the distraction they needed. Had Kian grabbing her arm, then pushing her behind him. He mouthed at her to wait, then darted out — waving Blake ahead of him as he blocked her from view then followed behind her. Both of them sprinting for the door.

They hit the exit still running, the door bouncing off the wall with a loud thud. Someone yelled her name behind them, but Kian already had Blake heading for some trees — ducking in behind them just as the men barreled out of the exit. Sweeping the area — guns at the ready. Faces twisted into snarls. They took a couple steps toward the tree line when Lane walked around the far corner of the building. And with how the exit was positioned, Lane wouldn't see them until they were face-to-face.

One second flat, and Blake was up and racing toward the other man. Either oblivious or unfazed by the bastards standing at the back door. That they'd see her pop out of the trees long before she'd reached Lane. What would likely get her killed.

Not happening. Not while Kian was breathing.

He pushed to his feet then took off after her. And he had to admit. She was fast. Arms pumping, feet flying — she'd covered nearly the entire treed area in a matter of seconds.

He caught her just as she cleared the small copse, matching her stride as he made eye contact with Lane. "Three tangos. Eleven o'clock."

That's all he got out before he had Blake in his arms — had her snugged beneath him as he took them both onto the grass.

Lane didn't disappoint. Had fired twice as he dove for cover, popping up close to them. The men shot back, clipping the tree next to Lane's head. Sending bits of bark spraying across the ground.

Kian managed a couple trigger pulls, as he jumped to his feet, Blake still in his arms. She didn't speak, running with him when he headed for the side of the clinic, Lane covering their retreat.

His buddy joined them a second later, dirt and grass staining his shirt. He changed magazines, nodding toward a long outbuilding at the edge of a larger stand of trees.

Kian gave Blake a quick once-over, then they were off, again. Staying low and over to the side in the hopes of remaining hidden. They reached the edge of the large outbuilding then dodged behind it, following it around toward the far parking lot.

Lane stopped them at the other edge, peeking around the corner. "I know I clipped at least one."

Blake moved in beside him. "There's bound to be more."

To his credit, Lane merely nodded. "There always are. So, who are we up against?"

Blake's mouth pursed as she looked them both in the eyes. "Does it matter?"

"I'd like to get a sense of the kind of skill we're facing."

"I highly doubt any of them will be ex-military. Their loyalty only goes as far as the money."

"So, mafia, then?"

She paused, eyes darting back and forth. She glanced at where they'd left the men, cursing quietly under her breath. "Mafia. Hitmen. Disgruntled family members. Take your pick."

"Your family's trying to kill you?"

"Not mine, Lane. And now's not the time for questions. I'll explain later... If we're still breathing."

As if on cue, footsteps pounded the pavement off to their other side. Lane shoved Blake behind his back, covering one side as Kian guarded the other. They weren't quite boxed in, but it wasn't ideal.

Blake held out her hand. "I need one of your spares."

Lane looked at Kian then arched his brow. "You know how to shoot?"

She simply stared at him.

Kian nodded when Lane silently asked him what he thought, then the guy handed her the weapon from his other holster.

Blake took it, checked the clip, cleared the barrel, then cycled a round, and damn, she looked way too comfortable with it. "We need to get to the helicopter."

"They'll hear us the moment you fire up the engines."

"Machine's still warm. I only need a minute."

Lane scoffed. "That might be thirty seconds more than we'll get before bullets start flying. I'll lure them off. You two head for the machine. Just… Don't leave without me."

Blake gave him a swat. "Like I've ever left a crew member behind. And you should take Kian with you. I'll be fine."

"Right. Leave the target without backup." Lane held up his hand. "Nothing I haven't faced before. Go. I'll be right behind you."

Kian grabbed Blake's hand then darted out, weaving through the trees toward the far side of the area. Just their luck, the building was backed by highway on two sides. Not exactly prime cover.

Lane snuck out to their right, back toward the first group. He fired twice — downed one guy, and clipped another — then he was running. Drawing the rest of the men in his direction.

Kian pushed down the guilt. If anything happened to Lane because of a risk Kian should be taking...

Blake obviously shared his sentiment, mumbling under her breath as they headed for the helicopter. Kian stopped them once they reached the end of their cover, scanning the area then waving her ahead. It didn't look as if the men had found her machine yet. Though, having them show up explained why Blake had parked in the back corner of the property instead of the cleared area next to the parking lots. She must have been worried someone might find her and had hidden the chopper as best as she could.

Kian stood guard as Blake jumped in. She did a few preliminary checks without making any noise then looked up at him. He nodded, staying vigilant as the helicopter sprang to life, the telltale whine of the engines likely to bring every tango right to them.

Ten seconds in, and shots sounded off to the right. Not so close Kian saw who'd fired them, but close enough it was only a matter of time before they were charging at him and Blake. Another ten, and Lane came racing out of more trees, hoofing it toward them. Kian fired off a few rounds when two men tried to follow Lane, sending both guys diving for cover.

Lane continued to the chopper, jumping in the back as Kian climbed in beside Blake. He didn't know if she was ready, but they were already out of time.

Whether she'd skipped some of the steps or had managed to get everything online, quicker, Kian wasn't sure, but she had the bird airborne a moment later. A tilt of the rotors and they were screaming toward the men pushing to their feet.

They dove, again, barely rolling clear before Blake soared over them, then banked it hard to the right. Kian swore the skids hit the trees before they were climbing, a couple shots pinging off the back end.

Blake followed some dry riverbed, heading for the water, when one of her instruments chirped. She glanced at the panel, touching a couple of the screens before keying up her mic. "Looks like we've got company."

Kian twisted in his seat, scanning the horizon until he zeroed in on a dark silhouette not too far behind them. "They have a chopper?"

"I doubt it's theirs. More likely some lowlife smuggler on their payroll. Not that it matters."

She tapped another screen, moving the display a bit before she smiled — glanced at Lane, then over to him. "Buckle up, boys. This is where it gets interesting."

8

In all the possible scenarios Blake had run through, this hadn't even made the list. Russo's men showing up at the clinic had been unfortunate, but nothing out of the ordinary. While she'd hoped Waylen had preempted the situation before the video had gotten any traction, she'd been prepared for this kind of scenario since she'd agreed to testify. Knew it meant she'd always be looking over her shoulder. But she hadn't realized Henry had the kind of connections to garner air support this far from home. A mistake that might cost Kian and Lane their lives.

Blake settled in, scanning the instruments as she headed for the coast. She didn't know who was flying, but if they wanted a fight, she'd give them one.

She keyed up the mic, praying Lane was a good

as Kian had claimed. "Lane, there's a rifle stashed in a lock box right below your seat. The code's zero, four, one, eight."

The day when everything had changed. When her life had gone up in smoke.

She waited until he had the weapon out before continuing. "There are extra magazines in that box. You can slide that one window open and fire out of it if the opportunity arises."

Lane grunted. "An M4. Why am I not surprised. It's standard issue for most agencies, assuming you aren't part of this cartel."

"I already told you. Not my family."

"You're just running from them, then." He hadn't asked, and she didn't answer.

"Stay sharp. If I do this right, maybe you won't have to fire, at all."

He snorted because he obviously knew she was lying. That it always came down to firepower.

Blake let it go, focusing on the shoreline quickly approaching out the front. She'd get low — hug the rocks. Use every trick she'd learned over the years chasing gun boats and drug runners in the hopes of out maneuvering whoever was flying the other machine. And if that failed, she'd put her faith in Lane, and they'd go on the offensive.

Her cell buzzed, vibrating in the holder off to her right as Porter's name flashed on the screen.

Nothing that broadcast his vocation, just the initials AP.

Kian glanced at it, frowning when she allowed it to go to voicemail. Now wasn't the time to talk. Not with the other machine bearing down on them.

She banked hard once they reached the coast, getting low enough Kian and Lane could count the pebbles on the beach. Water sprayed out behind them, twin vortices trailing across the top of the ocean.

Kian inhaled, checking their six before nodding at her. "What's the plan?"

She snorted. "To not die."

Her phone buzzed, again, the same initials flashing on the screen.

He pointed at it. "I'm thinking that's important."

"He can wait."

"I'm betting he can't."

She glanced at him — aware he'd most likely worked out which scenario fit the situation. Just like Lane. The only wild card was whether she was one of the good guys or an ex-associate who'd double crossed them.

She hoped he and Lane would give her the benefit of the doubt, but even she had to admit, it looked bad. She hissed out a breath, hitting the button on her comms. "Now's not a good time, Porter."

An irritated huff sounded over the airwaves. "No time ever seems to be good with you, Blake."

"You're on comms, and I've got Kian Fox and Lane Benning with me. They can hear everything you're saying."

"That's unfortunate because we need to talk. There's been a development."

"No shit." She cursed when a series of pops ricocheted off the fuselage, the report of what she assumed was some kind of freaking mounted machine gun sounding around them.

"Blake? What the hell was that?"

"That development you mentioned. They're already here. I've got a freaking chopper on my tail, and it's not friendly."

"A chopper? How the hell do they even know where you are let alone have a helicopter, already?"

"That stupid video. Isn't that why you're calling? To tell me you got some kind of alert?"

"I'm calling because our friend escaped custody on a damn medical run seven hours ago. What video?"

"Escaped?" She forced herself to swallow past the giant lump in her throat. "Russo's free?"

"Jesus, Blake, no names. Christ, this is a shit show. Just… get your ass back to the hanger. I'll meet you there."

"You're on the island?"

"I was in L.A. on a joint assignment when I got

the news. Hopped the first flight out. So, lose that bogey and get your ass home."

"I'm working on it. But I'll meet you at the Brotherhood Protector's office. And no, that's not negotiable. And yeah, you know where it is. In fact, I'm betting you're there, right now."

She should have made the connection sooner because the more she thought about it, the more she realized that Hawk had probably been aware of part of her story. Maybe not the finer details — who she really was and that she was in WTISEC — but when she reran all her dealings with the man over the past eighteen months, it looked a lot like he'd been privy to more classified intel. Why she'd passed whatever vetting he did for any people he worked with, without so much as a pause.

Knowing Porter the way she did, he probably had some remote connection to the guy. Some cousin a few times removed who'd been a SEAL, too. Or maybe he'd called on one of her father's former associates in order to get a recommendation. Something that had made Hawai'i and the Brotherhood Protectors safe.

God, Porter had probably asked Hawk to keep an eye on her, as well. Make sure she was sticking to the rules. Wasn't engaging with any questionable people. For all she knew, Hawk had called Porter as soon as she'd left, to tell him he thought she might be in trouble. Not that it mattered, seeing as Russo was free.

That's what really scared her. The man was ruthless. Psychotic. And if she wasn't careful, she'd get Kian, Presley and everyone else killed.

She hit the comms, praying she wasn't sentencing them all to death. "Time to take stock. I'm never going to outrun this guy. And I have to admit… His chopper's a bit more nimble than mine."

Lane snorted. "And let's not forget about that machine gun."

She nodded. "That, too. But I'm betting he hasn't flown the kind of missions I have. And I'm confident he doesn't have anyone as skilled as you, Lane. Hold tight. At some point, I'm going to serve him up on your side. Feel free to use extreme prejudice."

Blake clicked off the comms then settled in. Porter was right. This was definitely a shit show, and she'd said far too much. But, there was no sense worrying about her cover when it was already blown.

A breath and a silent prayer, then she had that bird dipping even lower, that other chopper trailing close behind. She banked hard left, hugging the coastline. Huge rocky cliffs rose out of the ocean beside her, adjoining formations dotting the water.

She danced the chopper through the scattering

of outcrops, taking them up and over one rise only to drop into the opening on the other side. Nearly skimming the waves as she picked up speed before banking again. Doubling back the way she'd come.

The men grunted as she threw the machine one way, then the next, circling some of those outcrops. Birds squawked around them, getting dangerously close as she banked hard, then brought the helicopter into a low hover.

She waited, that other machine screaming past when the pilot misjudged her actions. And that was all the opening she needed.

A stomp on the pedal, a shift of the controls, and she was racing after them. Dogging every move the other aircraft made. More of those rocky islands appeared in front of them, and she knew the other pilot was going to try and use them the way she had — switch their positions, again.

"Get ready, Lane."

She swooped in low, going left when the other guy went right. Coming out slightly in front — Lane's window perfectly lined up. Lane fired off a number of rounds, hitting the rotors — making the other helicopter bank hard in order to avoid more damage. Not quite a victory, but it bought her some time.

She reefed up on the collective, quickly gaining altitude — nose pointed toward the sun. The machine shook, a few alarms springing to life. "Hold on, baby, just a bit higher…"

Kian said her name, but she ignored it, holding steady until she'd pushed the chopper as far as she could. A quick shift of the controls, and they'd spun — were screaming toward the ground.

The other bird climbed toward them, a virtual head-on collision in the making. She held steady, a few shots pinging off the gear when the other gunner started firing. Her cue to hit the spotlight — all but blinding the other pilot. A slide to her left opened up Lane's side, again. Gave the man a clear shot at their engines.

And Lane didn't let them down. A few trigger pulls, and black smoke poured out of the cowling, leaving a trail as the chopper dropped several feet, banking off in the opposite direction. It headed inland, following a road, the machine jerking through the air. A steady line of smoke trailing after them.

Kian keyed up the mic. "We're not going after them?"

She glanced over at him. "And risk they might have more backup wherever they're headed? I'd rather take the win and make a run back to the ranch. Before more assholes show up."

"Sounds like a wise choice. Besides, you've got that meeting with Porter." He made eye contact. "He's your handler, right?"

She laughed, but not because it was funny. She knew he would figure it out. "He's something."

Lane grunted into the mic, leaning forward in his seat. "I think it's a bit late to worry about protocol and secrets, don't you? Besides, *I'm* the one who's been leaving the trail of bodies…"

Blake winced at the tone, not that Lane was wrong. He was the one who'd had to take the shots — who'd kept them all alive. And he definitely deserved an explanation.

She glanced back at him, then over to Kian. Drinking in all that blue in his eyes because she knew as surely as the fact Henry Russo wouldn't ever back down, that Porter would move her.

"You're right. You deserve the truth, and I'll walk you through it once we reach the ranch. You're not the only two who are owned an explanation. And, if you don't mind, I'd like to spend the rest of the flight trying to figure out my next move because I know what Porter's going to say, and I'm not sure I can live with his decision. Not this time."

Kian's eyes widened before he cursed under his breath. He looked back at Lane, then met her gaze. "Shit. I got it wrong. This isn't an investigation gone sideways. You're not undercover. And Porter's not here to provide backup. He's here to pull you out."

"Wait" Lane tried to get as close to them as possible in the back seat. "What do you mean, pull her out?" He stared for a few moments, then inhaled, eyes as wide as Kian's. "Well, crap. Porter's a U.S. Marshal?"

Blake swallowed, nearly choked, because just hearing it said out loud... It brought back all the feelings she'd buried when she'd had to walk away from her career — from her life — three years ago. What had been necessary to survive. To face each day without endless regrets.

She tried to steady her voice, knowing she wasn't nearly pulled together enough for them not to notice the waver in it. "It's U.S. Deputy Marshal." She sniffed, pushing everything down as far as she could, hoping it might get her through. "Porter's a stickler for detail."

Lane shook his head. "Are you serious? Because we all know what that means."

Kian leaned over. "It means, you're in WITSEC."

9

*H*e should have known. Should have guessed by all the clues she'd let slip — the way she stayed in the shadows — Blake wasn't here on some grandiose mission. Wasn't secretly on an assignment with the Brotherhood Protectors or tracking down an international spy for one of the many federal agencies.

She truly was hiding.

WITSEC.

Though, if Kian was being honest with himself, a part of him *had* known. Had guessed it from the start. He simply hadn't wanted it to be true because it was the one scenario he might not be able to change.

I'm not sure I can live with his decision.

That's what Blake had said. Kian's small

glimmer of hope that she was having doubts, too. Was questioning if she could give up her life, here.

If she could give him up.

Because he didn't want to let her go. Wanted to list all the reasons why staying on the Big Island, with him and his team as protection, wasn't just her best option. It was the only one.

But, how could he ask her to stay — to trust in him and his buddies — when they'd only known each other a few weeks?

Sure, it felt like longer. As if he'd known her all his life. That instant connection they'd had. Maybe not the details, but he knew the important ones. That she was brave. Strong. Was willing to go to any lengths to help others. Which was why she was in this mess.

Russo.

That's the name she'd said to Porter. Not that Kian knew who this Russo bastard was, but he'd change that. Would have Waylen hack into every database from here to the east coast if needed. Though, she'd promised to explain everything, and she wasn't one to break promises.

Deputy Marshal Adam Porter hadn't spoken a word since they'd landed at the ranch. He'd merely ushered them into the Brotherhood Protectors' office, where he'd been on his cell, ever since. And judging on the tension straining his back, Porter wasn't happy with whatever was being said on the other line.

Kian focused on Blake. She'd isolated herself to the far side of the room. Had her arms wrapped around her chest as if she was afraid she might fly apart at any moment. She'd barely given Presley more than a nod, already distancing herself.

Porter finally turned to face them. He did a sweep of Kian's team — all the people Blake had insisted be included in the meeting. That she apparently owed an explanation to. Except Lane. His buddy had taken one look at Porter — at how antsy the marshal was just standing there, watching them land — and had announced he was going to be their overwatch until they had this mess figured out. That Kian could fill in the details, later.

The fact Porter hadn't even balked when Lane had grabbed the rifle then headed for the roof of the building told Kian everything he needed to know. And it didn't take a psychic to see Porter was anything but impressed with how the situation was unfolding.

Porter settled on Blake, one side of his mouth twitching. "Well, this is a mess." He held up a tablet and started the video, sighing as he shook his head. "I always knew you'd be the one to give me an ulcer. Your type just can't step back from the fight, can you?"

Blake straightened her shoulders, holding her

head high. Any hint of uncertainty gone. "I was answering a distress call."

"You could have left it for the Coast Guard."

Her mouth tightened at the mention of the Coast Guard. Not something everyone might notice, but Kian did. "The closest ship was thirty minutes away. Presley didn't have that kind of time."

"Or maybe, you just didn't want to let your new best friend down."

Blake glanced at Presley, then took a step toward Porter. "Screw you, Adam. I would have answered it regardless of who it was, and you know it."

"Except where that's not what you do, anymore."

"This isn't about what I do. It's about who I am." Blake glanced at Kian. One of the first times she'd made eye contact since they'd landed. "You can change my name. Change my location. But helping people is in my blood, as my dad used to say. And no one's changing that. Not even that monster."

"I understand how hard it must be to become someone new. Someone you might not even like, but we have rules for a reason."

"I've followed your damn rules. I stay in the shadows. I haven't contacted anyone from my previous life. Not once. I even avoid streets where I know there are traffic cameras, for god's sake. I don't go into stores that have CCTV. And on the rare occasion I've gone out for a drink with my *only* friend, it's to a place people aren't taking selfies, if you get my drift."

Blake rolled her shoulders, stretching her head from side to side. "But I'm not going to stand by when someone needs my help. If I were that kind of person, I wouldn't be in this mess. I would have caved to the bastard's threats long ago."

Porter merely shook his head, again, leaning his ass against the desk. "I knew letting you continue to fly was a mistake."

"Like you could have stopped me. No—" She cut him off with another step forward. "I gave up everything to put him away. My friends. My career. My damn life. I'm not giving up the one thing that's kept me sane."

"Which is why we're standing here, your face plastered on the wall of every connection he has, and his damn goon army on the prowl. Do you realize how poorly that interaction at the clinic could have turned out?"

"I had backup."

"Right." He turned to Hawk. "Thanks for letting me know she was hanging out with a bunch of ex-Navy SEALs. Exactly the kind of people who bring out the officer in her."

Hawk shrugged. "Who else is she supposed to hang out with? If Lane's crew isn't safe, then no one is. Besides, you wanted someone to keep an eye on her. No one better than a SEAL, Adam."

"Except where they seem to leave as much damage behind as she does."

"At least, we were there. Where the hell were you and the Marshal Service?" Kian stepped forward, moving in beside Blake. Ignoring the way she snapped her gaze to him. As if she hadn't expected him to take her side.

He gave her hand a squeeze, staying close enough Porter would know exactly where Kian stood. "You said this Russo guy had been running around free for seven hours before you finally rang her cell. Why didn't you call sooner? I mean, your agency *is* keeping tabs, right? Are actively looking for anything that might put the people under your care at risk? Or did you just dump her here, read off a laundry list of impossible rules when every damn person has a cell phone, these days, and hope for the best?"

Kian glanced at his crew, smiling inwardly when they all gave him a nod. Confirmation they were as invested as Kian and had no plans of standing down. "I want to know who this Russo asshole is, and why he's trying to kill Blake."

"And this is why we don't divulge names, Garrett." Porter gave Kian a once-over. "I assume you're Kian Fox." He made direct eye contact with Blake. "The boyfriend."

"What I am, is someone who gives a damn. So, we can either stand here and have a civil discussion about threat levels, next steps, and what you're going to do to ensure Blake's safety, or I can get my buddy Waylen to hack his way into whatever secure database we need to uncover it all for ourselves. Your choice… Marshal."

Blake tugged on his sleeve, looking as if she was about to cry as she shook her head. "Kian…"

"I understand why you had to keep everything secret. That it was for our protection as much as yours. But the secrecy stops, here. Your cover's blown, and the wolves are already at the door, sweetheart. So, talk to me. What happened?"

Blake pursed her lips, eyes glassy before she tiptoed up — gave him a gentle kiss. That kind that said she was already gone. She brushed her thumb along his jaw, forcing a smile. "I love that you want to help. I do. But if I leave now, there's a good chance Russo's men will follow. Take that bullseye off your back. Not that I want to go. I don't, but… I can't lose…"

She didn't finished, closing her eyes as her head drooped forward.

Kian tugged her against him. He knew she'd fight him. Not because she didn't think he could help, but because she cared. Didn't want him to get hurt.

He gave her a few minutes to collect herself,

then eased back, tucking some of that silky hair behind her ear. "How about I make you a deal? You tell me about Russo, and I promise to back off if you leaving is the best option. Okay?"

She snorted, and he knew she'd figured him out. That there wasn't a chance in hell her leaving was ever going to be the best option.

Blake snagged her bottom lip — a rare moment when her bravado seemed to slip away. Left the vulnerable side of Blake standing there. "I…"

"How about I start?" Waylen looked up from the computer terminal he was seated at. Not that Kian had realized his buddy had sat down while they'd all been talking, but it made sense. "Russo. Henry James. Third generation mafia and head of one of the most notorious drug cartels in the Miami area. Suspected of drug trafficking, weapons dealing, and a large prostitution ring. Apparently both the FBI and the DEA had been trying to make a RICO case against his family for years, but couldn't get any traction. Then, two years ago, he was convicted of murdering three federal agents and is currently serving two consecutive life sentences at U.S. Penitentiary Coleman II."

Waylen arched a brow. "Seems they missed the part where he recently escaped his incarceration. And that's just a simple search. Imagine what I can uncover when I actually try."

Porter carded his fingers through his hair. Eyes

narrowed. Lips pursed tight. "SEALs. I should have known you'd gravitate toward your own, Blake."

Waylen grinned at Blake. "So, you are ex-military. Just like Hawk thought."

Hawk held up his hands when Porter glared at him. "Don't put this on me. I simply said I would have guessed she was military based on her skill. It's not like you told me any details, either. Just that she was scary good in a cockpit and to note if anyone questionable came looking for her."

Porter didn't even try to avoid confirming it. "Her branch is technically sectioned under Homeland Security. But close enough."

Kian grinned. Now it all made sense. "Endeavor to do more."

Blake eased out of his arms, staring up at him. "What did you say?"

"It's what you said when I asked if you were still okay performing the rescue when that storm kicked up. Was tossing us all over the place. I didn't hear half of it because the headset cut out for a bit. But that's what it was. Endeavor to do more, rather than less. It's part of your creed."

Raider stepped forward. "Well, I'll be damned. You're a puddle pirate."

Blake laughed, then held her head high. "That's Lieutenant Commander Puddle Pirate to you, squid."

"Puddle pirate?" Presley stared at Blake, eyes wide, mouth slightly open. "You're Coast Guard?"

Blake merely nodded. "For fifteen years. Right out of college."

Raider chuckled. "Now, everything makes total sense because you Coasties are hands down, the craziest SOBs I've ever met. You actually capsize those self-righting boats just for the experience."

Blake smiled. "Learning not to panic takes practice."

"I'm familiar. Wait… I had a buddy who did some joint operational work with one of the Coast Guard's TACLET units…" He glanced at Presley. "It stands for Tactical Law Enforcement Teams. Anyway, he did a few tours and said there was this badass pilot who was so skilled, they all started calling her Crossroads. Was rescued, himself, by that very pilot one night in the midst of a storm with only a flashlight to signal the chopper. Against orders, no less."

Raider grinned. "I don't suppose that was you?"

Blake beamed. Actually beamed, and Kian knew *this* was the real Blake. Not the woman who'd given up everything in the name of justice. Who kept to herself. Stayed on the sidelines. But the one who'd dedicated her life to the service.

She glanced around, some of that tension easing from her shoulders. "If I didn't know better, I would have thought Waylen came up with that dumbass name, just like he did nicknaming Kian, Ancient. Damn thing stuck, too. Took me years to lose it."

"Ouch." Waylen placed his hand on his chest. "Just like a Coastie to go straight for the jugular."

Presley frowned, brows furrowed. "Why did they call you Crossroads?"

Raider laughed, again. Louder. Deeper. "Because they all figured she must have made a deal with the devil in order to get that good."

"You Navy jackasses are all the same." Blake shook her head. "And I did get a reprimand for that rescue. A permanent stain on my record, I believe the Navy commander said. My CO didn't care as much because he preferred doing the right thing rather than necessarily following the rules. And it wasn't as if that was my first reprimand. Or my last."

Presley walked over and gave Blake a light swat on her arm. "I can't believe you were former Coast Guard — Lieutenant Commander to boot — and never said anything."

"I couldn't say anything. That's the number one rule of WITSEC. Whoever I was before I arrived on the Big Island didn't exist, anymore."

"Which is why I never should have let you keep flying." Porter held up his hand. "I know. It's in your blood. It's also what might get you killed."

Kian scoffed. "Not on my watch. Now, back to Henry Russo."

Blake pursed her lips, again, most of the color draining from her face. And Kian didn't need to be a rescue combat medic to know the beginnings of a PTSD episode when he saw one.

He took the two steps separating them, drawing her against his side. "Breathe, sweetheart. Everything's going to be okay."

She nodded. Way too fast to be believable, but at least she took a few quick gasps. Didn't look as if she might pass out any second.

Porter sighed, leaning against the desk, again. "Fine. Broad strokes. Three years ago, Blake was working out of the Coast Guard station in Puerto Rico. She was returning from a rather involved search and rescue mission when she received a report of a vessel in distress not far from the San Juan base. She responded along with one of the vessels. Long story short, they intercepted a drug smuggling boat and managed to salvage it and its contents and crew before they were lost to an inbound storm. By the time they towed the damaged boat back to the port, the storm had increased to a potential typhoon, and Blake was forced to park on the helipad at the main base until the worst of the storm passed and she could safely reposition her machine back to the air station. Perhaps you should relay the rest, Blake."

Blake nodded, still looking like a fucking ghost. "I won't go into details, but we confiscated enough cocaine and meth to get all of Miami high, which is where the shipment was headed. Three DEA agents met a couple of the crew and were moving the crates into a storage facility so they could catalogue everything."

She paused to take a breath. "I had just secured the helicopter when I heard a series of dull pops. But with the wind and the rain, it was hard to place exactly what they were, so I decided to double check. I rounded the main building when everything went for shit. There were shots and shouts — engines revving followed by the sound of metal scraping along the pavement. I hit the lot at a full sprint but…"

She swallowed, coughed, then tried, again. "Christ, it was chaos. All the officers were down. There was blood everywhere. A bunch of perps dressed in black with body armor and assault rifles were fanned out across the asphalt while others loaded the drugs into a couple of SUVs. I don't even know how the vehicles got there. If they busted through the main gate or broke through the chain-link fencing. Then, this man steps forward — aims a gun at the downed men and…"

Her voice trailed off. Just faded into nothing as she stared at the floor, paler than before.

Kian squeezed her hand. "You didn't simply call it in and wait for backup, did you?"

"There wasn't any time to wait for backup. Not

that it mattered. Three of the men still died and I…"

Porter blew out a raspy breath. "What Blake always neglects to relay is that, despite being outnumbered and outgunned, she took on the entire contingency of men. Alone. Got hit twice during her suicide race across the lot. But even wounded and bleeding, she managed to down four of Russo's men and provide life-saving first aid to two of the DEA officers when Russo's crew buggered off. We assume they thought Blake was the first of a contingency of officers headed their way. Unfortunately, the long-lasting effects from their injuries prevented the DEA agents from being able to testify."

Kian nodded, still holding Blake's hand. "But the man you saw kill those other officers was Henry Russo. And you testified against him."

A bit of color slashed across her cheeks. "The bastard murdered my teammates. Right there, in front of me. Of course, I testified against him. Wanted to burn his entire operation to the ground. Not that it turned out that way."

Porter shook his head. "We'd hoped that being on a secure base meant Blake would be safe from any kind of retaliation. But Russo's reach is ridiculously long, and after a couple failed attempts on her life that landed some of Blake's other crew members in the hospital, we had no other choice but to place her in protective custody until the trial was over.

Even then, we moved her as often as we could, hoping the Russo family might lose interest. But that never happened, so I called in a favor with an ex-military buddy of mine. He works for Hank Patterson's Montana division. Hank was actually the one who suggested I place Blake in Hawai'i, and I agreed that it seemed removed enough we thought she'd be safe."

Kian glanced at Blake, noting how she looked everywhere but at them. "But you think this video brought them all here? Is the reason Russo busted out of jail? Even though it didn't even go viral?"

"Like I said. Russo's reach is ridiculously long. And now that I've seen that damn vlog? Hell, yeah. I think one of Henry's contacts saw it, reported it back to him, and the bastard manufactured a medical emergency so he could break out then come here and personally get his revenge. Which is why we need to go. Before they turn this whole island upside down."

"Go?" Kian was in Porter's face before the man could blink. "Go where?"

"I'm sorry, but I can't tell you that."

"But you're going to provide twenty-four-hour protection, right? A group of marshals in a safe-house until this bastard's caught and you dismantle his organization."

Porter didn't need to answer because Kian knew they were simply going to ditch her by the way the man's mouth twitched. How he glanced at Blake then back to him. "We have a system in place—"

"Which is agent-speak for dumping her in some two-bit hotel and hoping Russo doesn't find her, again."

"I've got clearance to spend the next few days with her until we've got her new cover firmly established."

"A few days? Russo's still hunting her after three years and you think a few days of protection is what's going to be the difference, this time?"

Blake grabbed Kian's arm, pulling him back a step. "Kian. I know it sounds less than ideal, but the Marshal Service has thousands of witnesses they need to protect. Ones who haven't even gone to trial, yet. And all against men as dangerous as Russo. That's where they need to put their resources. My job's done. I just didn't realize he wasn't the only one getting life without the possibility of parole."

Porter scoffed. "Blake—"

"Don't. I don't regret the choices I've made, but it's true."

"I wish there was another option—"

"There is." Kian met Porter's narrowed gaze.

"What, you?"

"It's what we do."

"Correct me if I'm wrong, Fox, but you're

retired, and you don't even work for the Brother-hood Protectors."

Kian glanced at Hawk, raising a brow.

Hawk chuckled. "I've been meaning to have a formal chat with all of you about that. It just so happens, I'm in need of a team. And since Lane's on overwatch, maybe you'd like to speak for your crew, Kian? Let me know if the five of you would consider joining."

Kian looked around the room, grinning at the nods his teammates gave him. Not that they hadn't already been discussing it, but Blake's situation had definitely brought everything to a head. "We'd love to." Kian focused on Porter, again. "There, now we do."

"Mr. Fox—"

"That's Lieutenant Fox, U.S. Navy, retired, Deputy Marshal Porter."

"I don't care how you phrase it, this isn't a joke. If you get involved, and I mean really involved, Russo will target you and anyone remotely close to you, too. The man's a monster."

"Then, I guess it's a good thing we've all spent the past twenty years dealing with those."

"Kian." Blake pulled away, taking a moment to look at each of his buddies. "I can't ask you to do this. Adam's right. Russo's crazy. We got lucky at the clinic. We won't get lucky, again."

He took a breath, letting everything settle. Especially when after hearing the story, he had a nagging suspicion Russo's men were there to grab her, not kill her. That they were gunning for him and Lane because Kian bet his ass Russo wanted to finish this personally. "We don't need luck."

"And if he hurts Presley? Or Cassie?"

"We'll keep them out of the picture until we get a handle on how this is going to play out. What kind of resistance we're facing."

"What we're facing is an endless army of mafia henchmen. It's like that creature where you cut off one head and two more grow back. You said you'd let me go if leaving was the best option."

"Yes, I did. And if Porter can look me in the eyes and swear you're going back into full lockdown until they either catch Russo's ass or put him in the ground, then I'll help you pack your bags." Kian paused to meet Porter's gaze. "But he can't, and you being without backup, whether it's in Seattle, Tulsa, or fucking Anchorage is *not* the best option under *any* circumstance."

"Oh, for fuck's sake." Waylen pushed his way forward, stopping beside Kian and Blake. "This isn't about best options or protocol. This is about my best friend being stupid in love with you, Blake, and not wanting to lose you. So, either tell him you don't feel the same, and never could, or put the man out of his misery and accept our help. Your move."

10

*B*lake stared at Waylen. Had he really just claimed Kian was in love with her? Because it had sounded that way. Which was crazy, wasn't it?

She glanced at Kian, fully expecting him to roll his eyes. Maybe give Waylen a shove. Something to show Kian was just as surprised by the statement as she was. That his buddy was the one being stupid. Having Kian smile down at her, those gorgeous blue eyes of his practically sparkling in the light took her breath away. Or maybe it was the realization that he wasn't the only one who'd fallen in love. That she was right there with him.

Kian chuckled. "Breathe, sweetheart. Waylen's an ass, and this isn't how I pictured confessing anything, but he's not wrong. I am stupid in love with you — from the way you scrunch your nose when you think I'm crazy, to the fact you're willing to put your life on the line to save the people you care about, there's no denying it. And I hope the fact you're standing there, speechless, means I'm not the only one."

He'd spoken. She knew he had. His mouth had moved, and words had echoed around her. But she'd lost track of everything after he'd said Waylen hadn't been wrong and that he loved her.

Kian leaned down — dropped a chaste peck on her mouth. "Blake?"

An answer. He wanted an answer, but she couldn't quite remember the question.

She blinked, lifting her hand to rest on his jaw. "You love me?"

Kian shook his head. "If I'd known that was all it would take to throw you off your game…"

"Kian…"

"Yes. I love you. And I know… It hasn't been that long, and you have monsters in your maze — probably a laundry list of other secrets hiding beneath the surface. But that doesn't change the fact I can barely breathe every time I look at you." He brushed his thumb along her jaw. "It's okay if you haven't reached my level, yet. I don't expect you to say anything, but if there's even a chance you might—"

She kissed him. Right there in the Hawk's office. His buddies gathered around. Porter watching them as if he thought they were all nuts. And hell, they probably were. Signing up to become targets of one of the deadliest drug lords Miami has ever seen. The man who hadn't even blinked at killing federal agents. And all because Kian had fallen for her.

Though, she knew, even if he hadn't, they'd still offer to protect her, because they were heroes. Warriors who jumped into the fray without any consideration to their own well-being.

Champions.

Blake smiled when she finally eased back, still holding Kian's jaw. "I knew you were trouble the moment I saw you. And I'm edging more toward crazy than stupid but..."

Kian inhaled, held it, then let it all rush out in a raspy laugh as he grinned. "Hell, yeah, you are. Which means, no more running. No..." He stopped her from interrupting. "I know you're scared we'll get hurt. That you'll have our blood on your hands. But I need you to trust me. Trust my team. We can handle Russo and anyone he sends after you. Promise."

He turned to Porter. "I understand you have protocols. That your hands are tied and making her disappear is all you really have at your disposal. But you said it, yourself. This bastard's a monster. And no one should have to face that alone."

Porter stood there, glancing between them for so long Blake wondered if he'd had a heart attack but hadn't fallen to the floor, yet, before he muttered something under his breath. "Make that a bleeding ulcer. And yes, *Lieutenant*, we have a system. One that hasn't resulted in a witness dying, yet. Not as long as they follow the rules. The video was unfortunate. But moving her is still the best solution. Even with Russo hounding her. Now, if you're determined to stay by her side, I can look into you joining her in WITSEC, but your blanket assurances haven't changed my mind or my recommendation."

"Whoa, easy folks." Harlan moved out from the back, stepping between Kian and Porter. "Let's try to remember we're all on the same side and want the best possible outcome to the situation."

Blake shook her head. "There isn't anything to discuss. And while I don't want to be the reason anyone in this room gets hurt, I can't go through moving, again. I'm sorry, Adam. I know you're the only reason I've lived this long. But I just can't..."

She paused, gathering her strength to say the words she'd never thought she'd utter. "If that means I have to leave WITSEC—"

"Hold on a second, Blake." Harlan turned to face her. "Let's not make any rash decisions while everyone's emotions are high. Time to take a breath, then, we'll talk it out. Kian..."

Kian clenched his jaw but nodded, hooking her arm and gently leading her back to where Waylen and Presley were standing with Raider and Hawk.

Kian didn't speak, just kept her close, occasionally glancing over at Harlan as he spoke to Porter. Not loud enough she could hear what the men were saying, but it was evident Porter wasn't all that pleased.

Raider gave her a nudge. "While Harlan's stoic attitude can drive us all crazy, he's the best damn negotiator I've ever met. If anyone can calm this down, — help find some common ground — it's him."

Blake worried her bottom lip, wincing when Porter glared at Harlan, making some motion with his hands in what she suspected was an attempt to get his point across. "Maybe Porter's right, and I should just leave with him—"

"No way. I..." Kian took a visible breath. Looked as if he was counting to ten before slowly exhaling. "You're the one who's giving up every-thing. Who will have to leave your life behind, again. So, if you think relocating is the best option — what will bring some semblance of peace — then we'll leave. Go wherever Porter thinks is best. He has a point. The Marshal Service are pros at this, and the last thing I want is to pressure you into making a decision you'll regret."

"We?" She glanced around at his friends, but for once, they all looked like Harlan. Stone cold. "You can't just leave your team. Not when you've been telling me from the start that you guys agreed you'd find a way to stick together. And it's clear the island's become home."

Kian nodded. "You're right. We did, and it has. But not if you're not here. Because as much as I love these assholes — would do anything for them — I've come to realize, I love you more. And no, I'm not joking, and I'm not crazy. Like I said, I know it's been insanely quick, but I don't need to spend the next three years with you to figure it out. I've spent my entire adult life knowing whether a decision was right or not before I jumped out of the plane. And I can honestly tell you, I'm ready to jump." He leaned in, brushed his lips across hers. "You had me with that first kiss."

Was she crying? Drooling? Had she passed out and this was all a dream? Because she swore Kian had just said he loved her more than his brothers. That he'd leave, for her.

A press of his mouth across her forehead snapped her back, and she stared up at him, wondering what she'd done to deserve him.

She gave him a light shove. "No fair. Getting all charming on me. And no. I don't want to leave. Not when Russo will find me, again. And then what? How many times will the marshals relocate me? Us? How many last names do I have to go through before it's over? Not that it'll ever be over. Not while Russo's breathing."

She gave each of his teammates a hard stare.

"And no, that wasn't me asking you or your buddies to kill the guy. I still believe in justice. I just don't know how to have a life and not put everyone I care about at risk."

Raider inched forward. "How about you let us worry about the risk, and you find a way to get Marshal Porter on board. Because we could use a man of his expertise on this."

"That's Deputy Marshal." Porter moved into the opening Kian's team made for the man, Harlan standing slightly behind him. "You know, if I'd had any idea what a giant pain in the ass SEALs were, I never would have placed Blake here. And since when do your teams have a freaking negotiator? That seems like overkill to me when you've already got all the cool toys."

Kian grinned. "Harlan's special."

"Oh, he's special, all right." Porter ran his hand through his hair. "And he's raised some interesting points. So, let's cut through the bullshit and get down to tactics. While I'm not ready to toss out the idea of moving you, yet, Blake, I agree that in this particular situation — with the level of threat against you — the usual protocols aren't enough. Kian's right. You shouldn't have to face this alone, and I can only stay a few days. A week, tops. So, for now, I'll agree to alternate arrangements while we fully assess every option. That doesn't mean staying on the Big Island permanently will be my recommendation, but I'm willing to see if there's a way to make it work while providing you with the highest level of security."

Porter eyed Kian. "I just hope you and your teammates are as good as you think because this is definitely a war."

"The only easy day was yesterday."

Porter snorted. "So, I've heard. I'm also familiar with the phrase, abandon all hope, ye who enter here. Let's make sure that's not the one that ends up on our epitaphs."

"Great to know the Marshal Service is an optimistic bunch."

"Trust me. That's being optimistic." Porter nodded at her. "I'm going to assume since you haven't punched me in the jaw, yet, you're okay with having your boyfriend and his buddies accompany us to our next safehouse?"

She smiled. "You're coming, too?"

"After all we've been through, did you really think I'd walk away?" He shook his head. "All we need, now, is a plan."

Waylen stepped forward. "I've got an idea."

Kian groaned. "Please tell me this is better than when you thought scaling that mountain would save us days of traveling."

"It did save us days."

"Only because that damn rope ladder broke

while we were crossing the river and we got swept downstream."

Raider nodded. "I had to carry your pack because you cracked two ribs."

Waylen chuckled. "Good times. And this is much better. All we need are a couple boats—"

"Boats?" Porter shook his head. "No freaking way I'm trapping myself on a boat where the only alternate exit is jumping in the water."

"We won't be staying on the boats the whole time. They're mostly for transportation and to get us off the island without flying. Because I bet my ass Russo's people will be expecting Blake to fly out of here."

Porter mulled it over, finally nodding. "That's a fair point. But if we're not staying on these death traps, where—"

"Kian."

Blake inhaled as Lane's voice crackled over the handset clipped to Kian's waist.

Kian grabbed it. "Talk to me, Lane."

"We've got company. Four heavily tinted black SUVs bouncing along the gravel road. I can't confirm they're unfriendly, yet, but I'll bet my ass they aren't selling cookies."

"Roger. We're out of here."

Blake snagged Kian's arm. "There're too many people here. What if they don't follow us?"

Hawk stepped forward, already talking on his

cell. He paused for a moment, nodding toward the door. "You let me and my crew worry about the ranch. You just get someplace safe."

He tossed them all keys to the company's work trucks. "If nothing else, driving all the same make and color might confuse them. Stay sharp." Then he was out the door, yelling out that they needed more office supplies.

Kian took her hand, leading her outside then over to one of the white vehicles sitting in the driveway. "Hop in. Porter, you, too. We'll head out on some of the back roads. See if we can lose them."

Raider and Harlan jumped in another, while Waylen said he'd bring up the rear with Lane once Lane had provided some backup at the ranch. That they all needed to meet at the marina that night.

Kian nodded, revved the engine then took off. Dirt spraying out behind the tires as he barreled down the driveway, skidding onto an old two-track just past the barn then out toward the open fields. Raider's truck bounced along behind him, three of the four SUVs popping into view a few moments later.

Blake twisted in her seat, staring out the back. "I should have taken the chopper. Given you air support. Had them follow me, instead."

Kian chuckled. "You really aren't good with letting others take some of the risk, are you? And there wasn't time to get you to your helicopter and airborne. We'll lose them on the trails. Which reminds me… How did you get that chopper in the first place? Seems a bit odd the Marshal Service had a spare just lying around."

Blake grinned, glancing at Porter. "Guess it's a good thing they're in charge of asset seizure, then."

"It's a drug cartel chopper?"

"I think it was arms dealing, but close enough. But, she's mine, now, and I don't intend on giving her up."

Porter grunted. "Like I said. Bleeding ulcer. Fox, are you going to lose these bastards or what?"

Kian fishtailed the truck around the next corner, nodding at Raider when he pulled up beside them, then made a few hand signals — taking the next branching trail off to the right. "I just want to make sure we're clear of the ranch. That they keep following us. Then, we'll get serious."

One of the SUVs took off after Raider's vehicle, the other two sticking on their tail.

Kian passed a series of fence posts, then hit the gas. What Blake assumed was the boundary of anything to do with the ranch. The truck picked up speed, increasing the distance between them. Kian followed the winding path until they reached the next fork, then veered right, jumping onto an even rougher road.

The track dipped low then took them up a steep bank. Kian caught a few feet of air at the top, screaming over the edge, then down the other side. The back end fishtailing as the loose dirt sprayed out either side.

Blake held on, wondering if this was how Kian had felt when she'd been tossing the chopper around. If he'd been white knuckled, praying the machine didn't simply break apart. Kian didn't seem worried. Face relaxed. His gaze constantly dancing between mirrors.

He took the truck up the next large rise only to spin it a full one-eighty at the top. Made the whole vehicle slide sideways several feet, before the wheels caught on the gravel — kicked a bunch of stones off one side as they leaped forward. Heading back down the embankment.

Kian glanced back at Porter. "Now would be a great time for you to show us how good a marksman you are, Porter. Those assholes will be coming up on your side any second, now."

Porter already had his window open. "Like I didn't already know that. Just hold it steady for more than a second, if that's not too much to ask."

Kian glanced at her, rolling his eyes at Porter's comment before winking at her — the ass. She shook her head, inhaling when one of the SUVs came sailing over the rise, landing in a billow of dirt and stones, the chassis still bouncing as it careened down the hill.

Kian held the truck steady, racing at the other

vehicle — swerving to keep it on Porter's side. The marshal didn't disappoint, clipping the front passenger tire as they shot past each other, the SUV jerking hard to one side before flipping over — leaving a trail of debris across the ground as it tumbled down the rest of the incline, finally stopping in a heap at the bottom.

Kian whistled. "Nice shot. Now hold on. The other won't be that easy."

Porter muttered something about how the first one hadn't been easy, and that Kian needed to hold the damn truck steady, next time. Though, Blake had to admit, the man was skilled. Shooting out the tire while the truck was bouncing along the gravel path, the cab tilted slightly to one side with dust and dirt swirling through the air. Definitely not the average hit.

Not that Blake thought there was anything average about Adam Porter. Still…

Kian slowed enough to spin the truck — get it heading the other way, again — before the next SUV barreled over the rise. It hit the slope going some insane speed, barely remaining upright as it raced after them. A few winding turns, then Kian had them slaloming through the trees and brush. Blake wasn't sure how he avoided all the branches — didn't wrap the front end around a trunk. But he managed it, shooting out the other side onto another trail.

The SUV shadowed them, losing a mirror when the driver clipped a branch — blew out the passenger window in the process. Some asshole in black leaned out the open space, rifle notched in his shoulder. Dull pops sounded above the crunch of gravel beneath the tires, a few bullets pinging off the flatbed.

Kian cursed when the next shot took out his side mirror. "Hold on. I'm going to get creative."

He slammed on the brakes, while spinning the wheel, executing a sharp ninety-degree turn. Barely missing a giant boulder rising out of the brush. He skidded around it, heading back through some scrubby undergrowth before spinning it, again. Rocking to a halt with Porter's side facing the dusty cloud.

Porter had half his body hanging out the open window, lining up where he obviously hoped the SUV would punch out of the dust. He held firm, firing off a few rounds when the vehicle appeared around a small tree. Slightly off to the right, but Porter simply shifted his aim — caught the thing three times in the grill.

Steam poured out of the hood as the driver veered right, plowing into a stand of bushes.

But Kian was already off. Spraying more dirt and stones out from beneath the wheels as the truck lurched ahead. He took the next small two track, angling them toward the volcanos.

He gave her a quick once-over, eyeing Porter in the mirror. "Everyone still in one piece?"

Porter snorted. "No thanks to your driving. I'm not sure I want to know what they teach you in the SEALs because that was crazy."

Kian laughed. "You think I'm bad. You're lucky you didn't ride with Raider. He takes evasive driving to a whole other level. Scary good with an emphasis on scary."

"I just hope how all of you are behind the wheel isn't indicative to our upcoming boat ride."

"I get the feeling you don't like the water."

"I don't like trapping myself. But... We should take the long way there, just to be safe."

Kian nodded, reaching over to give her hand a squeeze. "Don't worry. Raider can handle the other tango, and Waylen and Lane were staying behind to help Hawk. Everyone's going to be fine."

Blake simply smiled because if she thought, for one second, she was the reason anyone at the ranch got hurt — if something happened to Presley just for being there — she might start screaming and not stop.

She needed to end this. She just wasn't sure how to do that and not lose Kian and herself in the process.

11

"*I* gotta say. After riding with Kian and seeing the state of Raider's truck now that we're all here, I think I'll take my chances with Russo's men."

Kian grinned as Porter crossed his arms over his chest, shaking his head as he stared at the boats Waylen had waiting at the marina. The marshal had surprised Kian. Not only was the guy one hell of a shot, he appreciated the other man's sense of honor. How he'd instinctively kept his body between Blake and any possible threat from behind. The guy was impressive.

Kian only hoped their plan worked because he could tell by the firm line of Blake's back — how she kept worrying her lip between her teeth — she wouldn't last too long allowing all of them to share in the risk. Not with how she was staring at the graze on Harlan's arm. Kian had treated it — assured her that his buddy had gotten far worse during training, let alone in the field — but just the sight of blood had changed her. Made it real or maybe it had just brought all the years she'd been running to the foreground.

Either way, he needed to keep an eye on her before she found a way to sacrifice herself for them.

Blake must have felt him staring at her because she stopped talking to Porter and looked over at him. And the smile she flashed him... It was all sin and promise. How he envisioned he looked when he smiled at her. All that love from within bursting free.

He hadn't planned on admitting he'd fallen in love with her. Not so soon. Especially since they hadn't even made their way into bed, yet. What seemed like an old-fashioned way of courting. But then Waylen had called Kian on it, and he couldn't stare into Blake's eyes and lie. Couldn't pretend she hadn't grabbed him by the heart and not let go.

That he'd been thinking about forever since she'd stared up at him that first night in his room as if she'd finally found someone she could trust. Who was worth breaking the rules for. He hadn't realized it at the time, but even then, a part of him had known that moment had been the start of the rest of his life. The one with Blake in it to stay.

It really was crazy. How his entire life had changed in the past month. He hadn't been joking.

He didn't need to spend months or years with her before he knew she was the woman he wanted to spend forever with. Whether it was because of his newfound freedom or just all Blake — that she was sexy and smart and had as much honor as his team combined — he wasn't sure. Only that he needed to end Russo's threat to her, or he might lose his future before it began.

Blake walked over to him, wrapping her arms around him when he tugged her in close. Breathed her in. She didn't talk, just stood there. Holding him. Bringing everything into hard focus. How close he'd come to having her walk away. Run, again.

He dropped a kiss on her forehead, brushing her hair back from her face when she looked up at him. "It's going to be okay."

She snorted. "You keep saying that, and I keep thinking you're all nuts. There's still time for me to disappear. I've already put everyone in enough danger. I should—"

"Stop trying to push me away. Not going anywhere, sweetheart. Unless this is your way of saying you really don't have any feelings for me." He nudged her. "Nowhere near crazy, like you said."

Blake looked as if she might dump him on his ass, or maybe shove him into the water before she palmed his jaw — drew him down to her. "Way past crazy and on my way to ridiculously. But thinking I might get you or one of your buddies hurt, or killed…"

He kissed her. Not that now was the time to lose himself in the soft press of her lips. Or how she tasted like promise with a hint of coffee. But he needed her to realize he wasn't going anywhere. That they fought because it was the right thing to do — part of their DNA just like she'd claimed flying was for her. That they'd spent their lives protecting strangers. Nothing they wouldn't do for the people they loved.

A throat cleared behind them, Waylen standing there, smiling smugly. "You two just can't keep your hands off each other, can you?"

"Says the guy who's already an expectant father after only a few weeks with Presley."

Waylen laughed. "Thankfully, this is all about your messed up love life and not mine. Which reminds me. Blake, I swear if I have to come searching for you because you've ditched us, I'll have Presley name one of her boats Puddle Pirate. We're a team, which means we stick together. No *John Wayne* sacrifices at the eleventh hour."

He merely snorted at the glare she flashed him. "Please, we all saw the way you looked at Harlan because of that scratch he got."

Blake huffed. "He was shot."

"Grazed, and not even a bad one at that. And it doesn't take a genius to see how you're thinking running off on your own will save us. But we've dealt with threats far worse than Russo. So, do us a favor and help us catch this bastard."

"You're all certifiable. You know that?"

"Yup. But I think our brand of crazy is exactly what you need. Raider and Lane will take the first shift in the Scarab. The rest of us will use Presley's vessel. We'll probably break our own rules and run all night, but just to put some mileage between us and any assholes Russo has running around. We'll dock at my buddy, Mano's set of cabins on the south side of Maui tomorrow. Stay there for a day and evaluate our next move. Whether we cabin hop for a few days or make our way back here and do a few trips around the Big Island."

Kian nodded. "I'm sure Porter will have an opinion on that. Call me crazy, but I think it's more than trapping himself on the boat that's got him looking like he wants to take on Russo, right now. How much do you want to bet he's had an incident involving a boat?"

Waylen grinned. "Or, maybe he can't swim."

"Of course, I can swim. Don't be an ass, Brown." Porter moved in beside him. "And if you must know, I made the mistake of riding with Blake's crew on a fugitive recovery mission a couple months before her life went to shit. And I'm not too proud to say, her teammates were insane. I would have turned around just trying to get out of the harbor. The waves…"

"I told you to fly with me, but you thought I was too…" She grinned. "How did you put it? Intense, I think."

"You are intense. And way crazier than any other pilot I've ever met. Which is why you and your new friends get along so well." Porter shook his head. "Though, you're right, Brown. We definitely need *your* team's brand of crazy if we have any hopes of actually surviving this. And Blake… I will gladly shoot you, myself, if you try to ditch us."

Blake gave them all a sketchy side eye. "Why does everyone think I'm going to ditch you? Do I like putting your lives at risk? No. Do I think I can handle this myself? I'm not that naive. So, stop worrying about me stealing the Scarab or thinking I can swim to shore when we're five miles out."

She crossed her arms over her chest. "But know this… If it comes down to my life versus all of yours, I'm making the tough call. I suggest everyone here makes peace with that. Now, are we going to stand around talking all night and give Russo a chance to track us down, or are we getting our asses out of here? Sun's already going down."

Kian sighed, shouldering up beside Waylen when Blake struck off toward the boats. Head high. Back rigid.

Waylen whistled. "She is a thousand kinds of stubborn."

"It's probably the only reason she's still sane. I can't imagine how hard it was to give up her career, her life, knowing she'd always have a target on her back." Kian held up his hand when Porter glanced his way. "I'm not knocking what you do, Porter. In fact, I'm more than impressed. With the kind of threats you face with every case like this, I don't know how you keep everyone alive."

Porter shrugged. "Half skill, half dumb luck. And for the record, Russo's on a whole other level. Most of the mafia I've dealt with, eventually give up. Sure, if Blake had landed on national news for that rescue, I would have expected some retaliation. People who make it easy or leave, don't always get their happy ending. But having Russo orchestrate all of this from that obscure video? That was up for less than forty-eight hours? With just a blurry image of her at the end? No names. No specifics. I don't think I want to know how many people the asshole must have on his payroll searching for her. Which means, this ends. I know Blake wants justice to prevail, but the bastard had his chance. Now... We go to the mattresses."

Kian smiled. "I think we're finally starting to understand each other."

"Oh, I understood you from the start, Fox. I gotta admit. I didn't think Blake would ever let anyone inside her walls. You must be very persuasive."

"She's worth the effort."

"Just make sure your buddy, Harlan, doesn't get any bright ideas about negotiating with Russo. I'm really not interested in giving the man an out."

"I'll have a chat with him. Caution him on using his superpowers for good."

"Right. Now, are we doing this or what? Because I hate boats, and if we don't head out, soon, I'll change my mind."

Porter struck off, meeting up with Blake at the edge of the dock. He must have said something funny because she laughed, then glanced back at Kian. She gave him a hint of a smile, but it hit him full force. How her eyes softened, a hint of pink coloring her cheeks. She looked radiant. Beyond radiant, and he had to remind his damn lungs to inflate. Pull in enough oxygen that the black dots flittering across his vision eased.

Waylen knocked his shoulder. "God, you two are sickening. You know that, right?"

Kian glanced at his buddy. "If only you could see your dopey-eyed expression whenever you look at Presley, you wouldn't be one to judge. Which reminds me, I owe you an ass kicking for that stunt you pulled in Hawk's office. Telling Blake I'm stupid in love with her."

"Someone had to say it before she took off with Porter. And it's not like it isn't true."

"You were guessing."

Waylen snorted. "I really wasn't."

"Still a dick move."

"I think you mean brilliant because now you can finally make a real move. Just remember the walls are thin on the boat."

Kian shoved him. Hard. "You're an ass."

"The one you know and love. Though, apparently not as much as you love her ass."

Kian carded his hand through his hair. "Waylen."

"Don't. I'd already told everyone I was breaking ranks and staying on the Big Island even if they left because my life is here with Presley. And as much as it would have hurt to have the rest of the team leave…" He made eye contact. "To have my best friend leave, it would have hurt more to walk away from her. And frankly, not something I could have done and still kept breathing. I had to leave Presley once. It wasn't happening, again. So, I get it. We're family, but she's your forever. So, don't mess it up, or it's your ass I'll be putting a slug in."

"Like I'd let you sight me long enough to shoot me in the ass."

"Only takes a moment."

"You're good. But I'm better."

"Guess we'll find out if you fuck everything up."

"I won't." Kian took a few steps toward the boat. "And for the record, I would have stayed on the island, either way. Though, you would have owed me big time for planting roots next to a volcano."

"Then, I'm lucky it's Blake who'll owe you."

Kian glanced over at her, his damn heart stopping cold at the mere sight of her. Hair blowing in the breeze. That adorable chin held high. Pure defiance in the line of her back. She was gorgeous. "Pretty sure I'm the one who's in the red."

He motioned to the boat. "We should head out before I have to sedate Porter just to get him onboard."

Waylen clapped Kian on the back as he walked past, ushering everyone onto the boat. Blake made a fuss about how it was one of Presley's boats, and she didn't want her friend losing an asset if it got damaged, but Waylen simply shook his head as he readied the boat for launch.

Kian moved in behind Blake, placing his hands on her hips as he pressed his chest into her back — smiling when she relaxed against him. "I promise, we'll take really good care of everything. And Porter already said something about the Marshal Service covering any damages."

Blake snorted. "Which means they'll simply replace it with some cartel boat they've got sitting in storage."

"All the better. Then, she'll have a place to hide shit."

"Can you imagine Presley and Waylen as drug runners?"

"They'd be horrible at it. Too much damn honor." He nudged her. "Just like you."

She stiffened. "All I did was tell a bunch of people what I saw. You would have stopped Russo from killing my teammates in the first place."

"Sweetheart. You did everything you could. Got shot twice, according to Porter, while taking on what? A dozen mafia assholes? All by yourself? Which we should definitely have a chat about because that was insane. But it's not your fault Russo's a psychopath. And as good as I am — as my team is — we aren't infallible. We've lost teammates — brothers — all because we couldn't fire quick enough. Or get to them fast enough. That's the ugly part of our job — yours too."

He dropped a kiss on her neck, grinning at how her breath hitched before she tilted in order to give him more room. "Come on. It's been a long day, and I can't remember the last time any of us ate something."

"How am I supposed to eat when Russo might have an RPG and just blow the boat out of the water?"

Kian laughed. Damn, he loved her. "Not tonight. And we've got the Scarab for recon."

Blake looked at him over her shoulder. "Just don't die on me, okay? Russo's already taken everything I've ever loved. I can't lose you, too."

Kian lifted his hand — brushed his thumb along her cheek. "Men far more skilled than Russo have tried, and I'm still standing. But I'll be careful. Promise."

He closed the distance, teasing her with a hint of a kiss before sinking his fingers in her hair — claiming her mouth. She barely let him come up for air as she turned within his embrace, dragging him back down. It wasn't until a throat cleared behind them, Kian was able to ease back — register anything other than how soft her lips were. How fucking bad he wanted her.

Waylen tsked. "Just pick a room if you don't like the one I gave you, buddy, and keep the noise to a dull roar before you throw caution to the wind and pin the poor girl to the wall."

Blake glanced over at Waylen. "I should be so lucky."

Waylen shook his head. "And that's my cue to go see how Porter and Harlan are. Last room on the right has your names on it."

Kian groaned, tugging Blake against him as Waylen made kissing noises as he continued toward the stern. "Waylen's an ass."

"Maybe. But I meant what I said."

Kian would *not* spin and pin her to the wall in

the middle of the damn boat. He wouldn't. He had more control than that.

Until she smiled up at him, trailing one finger down his chest. "You *can* pin me to the wall, right?"

Kian clenched his jaw, reciting some old mantra as he leaned down — got within an inch of her mouth. "Guess we'll worry about food later because that was definitely a challenge, sweetheart, and I haven't backed down from one of those since I was five."

12

$\mathcal{B}$lake inhaled as Kian all but heaved her over his shoulder and struck off down the short corridor to the door at the end. The cabin Waylen said was theirs. He didn't slow at the threshold, simply pushed the door open, ducked through, then kicked it shut. A turn and a step, and her back hit the wall, Kian's massive form holding her against it.

He leaned in, their breath mixing as he stared at her. Nostrils flaring. His chest crushing against hers with every inhalation. As if he couldn't quite pull in enough air.

She couldn't. Already had flecks of black edging her vision simply being this close. Knowing where it was leading. Where she'd wanted it to go from the start but had been too afraid to lower her guard long enough to make it happen. Not that she hadn't trusted Kian. She had. Which was mostly the problem. She'd known from that first kiss in his hotel room, he was dangerous. That if she let him get close, she'd break ranks. Confide everything.

She just hadn't imagined he'd feel the same way. That despite being an ex-Navy SEAL — one of the last real warriors — he'd willing choose to go up against the likes of Russo. True, he had likely faced worse and come out the other side intact. But those had been missions. Choices he and his team had made. And she couldn't help but worry she'd somehow made this choice for him.

That her admitting she was ridiculously in love with him would be what got him killed.

Kian paused, as if he'd followed her internal turmoil and knew exactly what she was thinking. He leaned in — rested his forehead on hers. "While there's nothing I want more than to finally get the chance to make love to you, I realize this might not be the right time. Hell, the right head space. You're exhausted. Scared. And if you had any more guilt radiating off you, it could power the boat. So, if you'd rather wait until after we've dealt with Russo, I'll understand. And no, it won't change how I feel."

He eased back enough to brush one hand along her jaw while still keeping her pressed to the wall. "I fell this hard, this fast without us tumbling between the sheets. And while that might seem odd or insanely old-fashioned, it's true."

Obviously, resistance was futile. He already had her heart, and she knew he would until the day she died. She just hoped it wasn't in the next week. And she hoped she wouldn't take his team with her.

Blake managed to wedge her hand out from against his chest and palm his cheek. "What if it's not as earth-shattering as you think it'll be? What if I disappoint you?"

He laughed, the brute. "Sweetheart, you and the word disappoint do not belong in the same sentence. And you've already surpassed every expectation simply standing there, looking at me as if I've saved your soul. So, whether we spend the next few hours wrapped around each other, or we just sleep, I'm still going to be blown away having you in my arms." He nuzzled her nose, giving her a ghosted kiss. "Your move, puddle pirate."

Definitely futile.

"You're right. I am exhausted. Three years' worth of trying to monitor every second of every day. Constantly weighing the need to buy groceries or have a beer with Presley over whether it was smarter to stay home. And while I hate admitting I'm scared of anything, Russo terrifies me. I've seen what the man can do — how ruthless he is — and just thinking he could do that to you, or your team..."

She swallowed, nearly gagged, but managed to keep everything down. "And honestly, I'm not sure there'll ever be a good time or the right head space as long as he's a threat. But I don't want him ruling my life, anymore. Not where we're concerned. So, if you're still crazy — about me and this insane mission — then shut up, and show me what you've got, sailor."

Kian stared at her, eyes clearly assessing if she was being honest or simply saying something he might want to hear, before he smiled — slipped that hand on her jaw around to the back of her head. Threaded his fingers through her hair. "Pretty sure I passed crazy somewhere on the drive here. So, let's see if I can live up to your expectations."

Blake nipped at his bottom lip, kissing the slight hurt a moment later. "Then, mission accomplished. But, I'd love to see just how far you can push that bar."

"Another challenge. I think you should take a breath. Because I plan on stealing the rest of them."

She didn't even have time to tease him back before he'd claimed her mouth, again. Tangling his tongue with hers before kissing his way down her neck. He sucked at her pulse point — probably leaving a damn hickey as if they were teenagers — then nipped his way back to her mouth. Only this kiss shattered all the others. All lips and tongues, and by the time he eased back, she was already on the edge. Riding that fine line between wanting him inside her and wanting it to last for the next five hours.

Forget Russo killing her. Kian was going to give her a heart attack just from kissing her.

He must have realized how far gone she was, already, because he paused long enough to smile down at her. Allowed her to suck in some air when he'd stolen the rest, just like he'd said. Not that she cared. She'd find a way to breathe through him as long as he kept kissing her. Holding her.

A lift and a shift, and her shorts and panties were gone. Either puddled on the ground or maybe he'd ripped them off. He took a quick step back before tearing off her shirt and tossing it behind him without putting her down. His hand at her back had her bra joining the other clothes, nothing but the warm Hawai'i air brushing her skin. A smug smile, and her back was against the wall, again.

Blake inhaled while he yanked his shirt over his head — shoved his pants down to his knees. A quick flick of his hand to secure a condom, then, he was back. Hands palming her ass. Her legs wrapped around his hips.

He spent another several minutes teasing her — using one hand to explore every inch of her body before he seemed to reach some kind of limit. The one she'd blown past after that first kiss.

One last soulful glance, then he was thrusting inside, pushing her over that edge inside of a heartbeat. Eyes squeezed shut, she let her head fall against the wall — tried to lever some of her weight. Not that he seemed to notice. One minute in, and he had her chanting his name. Another five, and she was using every trick not to fly apart. Wanting it to last forever.

Kian nipped at her neck, smiling against her skin at her hushed moan. "This is just our first round. A quick romp to take the edge off, then... I *might* be able to focus long enough to play."

His voice. All low and gravelly. As if he'd had to work up the energy just to get the words out. Was as far gone as she was.

"God, Kian. I can't..."

Her confession only spurred him on. Had him upping his pace. Probably rocking the boat from the force. Creating some kind of massive wake. Or maybe it was just her that was off kilter. Whose world had been unhinged, leaving her with no other choice than to hold onto him for balance.

Was her back smacking the wall? Echoing through the entire berth? Had she just shouted his name as the fire in her core exploded, sending a billow of heat coursing through her body?

She didn't know. Frankly, didn't care. Not when Kian latched onto her shoulder — started emptying inside her. All that power still keeping her tight to the wall.

How they didn't end up in a heap on the floor

was a mystery. Likely the result of sheer strength or years of training. Regardless, she smiled against his neck, doing her best to tug him closer when he sighed, all the tension she'd felt in his muscles, finally easing.

His breath sounded in her ear, the raspy quality erasing any doubts he wasn't all-in. That he hadn't really meant it when he'd told her he loved her.

That this wasn't forever in the making.

A kiss behind her ear got her attention focused on his eyes when he finally lifted his head and smiled down at her. "Christ. That was supposed to be a quickie, but damn, I'm not sure I can move."

She laughed. It wasn't forced or because she thought it was what he expected. But because he'd eased the pressure around her heart. What she'd needed to keep going when she'd been alone. Vulnerable.

He'd lifted that. Given her a reason to step out of the shadows. Live the life Russo had taken.

"You did do all the work. So, how about I make it up to you and return the favor?"

And just like that, the heat was back in his eyes. Any hint of fatigue gone. Vanished like her clothes had.

Kian tsked, slipping free with a grunt. As if leaving her had hurt. He disposed of the condom, shucked the rest of his clothes, then picked her up. He spun, took the four steps over to the bed, then launched them both on top. They bounced once, the mattress creaking under the strain before he was looming over her. His hair teasing his eyes. All that blue staring down at her.

She reached up — brushed the silky locks back. "How did I get so lucky?"

"I'm the lucky one. You didn't have to let me in. I'm actually surprised you did."

"It's not like I had a choice. You had me from that first kiss, too. I just didn't know how to love you and not tell you everything."

His smile. It was sexier than ever. A hint of white between full pink lips. Laugh lines around his mouth. The man was beyond handsome. And he was hers.

"All the more reason to show you how much I appreciate that trust. Another deep breath, sweetheart."

"I believe I said it was my turn to do all the work."

"You did. And you can." He dipped down — claimed her mouth with a kiss that had her revved up into the red zone in a heartbeat. "Once I'm done with my turn. Which I don't think is going to happen until at least the morning. Or the next week. Possibly a month."

"Kian…"

He merely chuckled. "Shut up, and let me see how far I can push that bar."

God, how could she argue with that? Especially when he'd tossed her own words back at her.

"It's already pretty high, but…" She levered up enough to claim his mouth in a searing kiss. "Give it your best shot, sailor."

Another sexy smile, a brush of his mouth over hers, then he was trailing down, licking and kissing every inch. Making her giggle when he caressed the side of her breast only to turn it into a moan when he captured a nipple in his mouth — sucked on it.

He switched sides. Applying just the right amount of pressure, he had her arching off the bed — sliding her fingers through his hair. She gave a tug, but the man didn't stop. Didn't seem to realize how close she was, already. That he'd blown the bar into a thousand pieces, just like she was going to shatter into at any moment.

"Kian…"

A raise of his head, and an arch of his brow was the only response she got for another full minute before he finally moved down her body — wedged himself between her thighs.

She pushed her head into the mattress, fingers still gripping his hair — every nerve strung tight. Until he blew a heated breath across her flesh — had her nearly screaming his name. She managed to crush all but a harsh groan — saving them from having one of his buddies bust through the door wondering if they were being attacked.

Kian didn't seem to share her concern that Waylen or Harlan might hear them. Come knocking if they misunderstood the circumstances. Kian simply grinned against her skin then drew his tongue along her drenched flesh.

Dead. That's what she'd be in exactly five seconds. Once her heart exploded after pounding out through her chest. Or maybe she'd have an aneurism right there from the infuriatingly light flicks of his tongue. Licks designed to keep her perched on the edge. Waiting. She lasted maybe five minutes before she fisted his hair around her fingers and pulled sharply.

Kian chuckled, the bastard, before lifting his head. Raising an eyebrow at her as if he had no idea why she was ready to shove him onto his back and take matters into her own hands. "Something on your mind?"

Blake managed to push onto her elbows, not that it helped the situation. Seeing her thighs splayed around his massive shoulders only increased the need burning beneath her skin. Made her acutely aware she was seconds from going over, with or without him. "Either stop teasing me, or your turn is over."

Kian tsked. "Really, sweetheart? I thought you Coasties were all about patience?"

"We're about getting the job done, and I'm a second away from going over, whether you're ready or not. But if you want to rob me of my orgasm…"

"Ouch. Waylen was right. You do go straight for the jugular."

"Do you know how long it's been since…"

His eyes narrowed, and he levered up, closing the distance until he was an inch from her face. "I'd be foolish to think every man on this island hasn't been trying to get you like this. But I'll admit. My fragile ego wants to believe it's been a while. Just like me."

"If three years is your definition of a while, then…" She palmed his cheek, enjoying the stubble shadowing his jaw. "And no one's been where you are."

His gaze softened. "Another lethal hit." He smoothed his hand down her chest, across her stomach then between her legs. "Eyes on me, Blake."

Eyes on him?

How the hell was she supposed to focus on anything, let alone those gorgeous blue orbs that were staring at her as if she'd soothed some inner demons just by confessing it had been more than a while. That he was the first man she'd trusted since that fateful night. And she hadn't been joking. No one had ever held her heart the way he did. Which seemed as crazy as she was about him.

Kian paused, doing that weird head tilt as if he

was following her thoughts, again, before grinning smugly. Like he knew exactly how far gone she was. And she would have called him on it if he hadn't leaned down — kissed her as if she might break. Soft. Coaxing.

She held him tight to her, somehow managing to look him in the eyes as he took her to the brink, again, every swirl of his fingers inching her higher. She whispered his name, each increased breath fluttering the hairs teasing his eyes. Making them dance as that coil inside cinched tighter. She tried to stem the heat billowing through her core when Kian dipped down — captured her lips in a searing kiss.

She broke. Died. Probably incinerated on the spot as her release washed over her, lulling her into a numbing haze. It wasn't until he kissed her, again, that she managed to look up at him. Smile.

He chuckled. "Judging by the smile on your face and how you drenched my fingers, I'm guessing I didn't rob you, after all."

She sighed. "No one likes a sore winner."

"Pretty sure I wasn't the one who won this round."

God, she loved him.

Blake beckoned him back down to her with a shift of her head. "I won more than just the round. Now, kiss me, again, and make love to me."

13

He'd definitely won more than the round, too. And if he played his cards right, he'd have Blake in his bed — and his life — for the rest of his.

Kian glanced at his pants over in the corner of the cabin, trying to figure out how to grab a condom and not let go of her. Because despite his brain sending the signals, they weren't getting through. One hand drawing lazy circles on her hip, the other playing with the ends of her hair. And the way she was tucked up against him, all he needed to do was shift and he'd be perfectly lined up. Could be inside her, again, in five seconds flat.

Blake followed his gaze, then looked up at him, all bright blue eyes, her hair like a ring of deep embers around her head.

She was definitely a goddess.

She palmed his cheek, giving him a gut-wrenching smile. "I already trust you with my life, and I'm on the pill. Maybe we could forgo the condoms because I'd really prefer that there wasn't anything between us."

He moved. Shifted like he'd been thinking about and found himself fully inside her a moment later. Or maybe it had taken more than a second. He didn't know. Couldn't really remember anything after her saying she didn't want anything between them. That she trusted him.

Blake clutched his back, probably leaving tiny, finger-shaped indents in his flesh. But he didn't care because she was right there with him. Body strung tight. Her heels hugging the small of his back. And when he tilted his hips — pressed into her, again…

It was all warm, wet pressure pulling him under. Threatening to have him unloading in record time.

"God, Kian."

That did him in. Broke the fragile hold he had on any semblance of rational thought. A few minutes in, and he was already fighting not to finish. To make it last longer than what they'd already shared against the wall. The round that was supposed to take the edge off and allow him to show her just how amazing it could be between them.

He forced himself to pause — think of something other than how fucking perfect she was. How her body complemented his. Soft and strong at the same time.

Blake inhaled then sank her fingers into his hair — dragged him down for more of her drugging kisses. The ones he knew he couldn't live without. She smiled up at him, eyes rolling when pressed harder into her. "I need…"

"Me, too. Hold on."

He gathered her in his arms then dipped a shoulder. It took a bit to roll and not have them continue onto the floor, but he managed it. Grinned up at her once he had her straddling his thighs. Her hands palmed on his chest. "Your turn."

Blake's eyes widened, before she bit at her bottom lip, adjusting herself until she must have found the right position. A few tentative pulses then she was sliding up, pausing with him slightly inside her, then lowering, grinding her groin to his.

Three minutes in, and he was questioning his sanity. Why had he thought having her drive would give him more control? Allow him to last longer? But the way she moved — hair fluttering around her like a sea of auburn fire, every muscle contracting, creating a patchwork of shadows along her skin. It was like watching a sexual dance. And when she angled her hips, hit that spot just right…

Her head tilted back, exposing the sexy line of her neck as she moaned. He wasn't sure if it was his name or a few guttural syllables that sounded close.

He only knew that it had him levering up — trapping her between his chest and his legs.

He wrapped his arms around her, ravaging her mouth until she was panting. Looking at him as if he'd completely wrecked her. Taken her beyond some limit.

Kian froze, wanting to burn everything into memory. The flush of pink on her skin. Her lust-blown eyes. How every breath pushed her chest harder against his.

Blake leaned forward, nibbled his ear. "Back to you."

Hell, yeah, it was his turn, again. And he didn't waste it. A shuffle sideways, and he was able to spin — take her down on the bed. Bodies still joined. One hand holding her head. She wrapped herself around him, every inch touching. He'd thought about flipping her — taking her from behind, but he needed her like this. Gazes held. Her lips within easy kissing distance. And after their quickie against the wall, he wanted her comfortable. Safe.

Blake didn't seem to care if he was squishing her into the bed or if her hair was stuck beneath her. She simply attacked his mouth — tried to urge him deeper with a firm press of her heels. Kian intended on telling her, no. How he wanted to make it last. Make it special.

Until she nudged him, again, as she lifted into

his small thrust. Took him back to the brink in under a second.

Gone. That's what he was. Lost in her.

He started moving. Slow then faster, increasing his pace until he was pounding into her. Thrusting so hard the springs were squeaking. The whole room rocking. Or maybe it was the boat cutting through the water. Either way, he was riding that high minutes later, his release burning down his spine. Blurring everything into the feel of her skin against his. The rasp of her breath against his neck.

Blake tensed, pushing her head into the bed as she cried his name, her body convulsing beneath him.

He managed to stop long enough to watch her tip over — that flush burning deeper as sweat beaded her skin, her body shaking. Then, he was coming. Hips jerking, every muscle contracted. The room faded into black, Blake's hold on him the only thing keeping him from floating away.

The room was dark when he finally pried his eyelids open — looked around. Blake's eyes were shut — was already halfway asleep.

Kian gave her a gentle shake. "Hey, beautiful. You need to eat something."

She huffed, tugging him near, not that he thought they could get any closer to each other. "Later. Roll over and hold me."

"How about I help you up, give us each a quick

wipe down, then grab some food and feed you in bed?"

That got one eye slivered open. "You'll do all the work?"

"It's still my turn, right? You did relinquish yours when you said it was back to me. So, yeah, I'll do all the work."

Blake stuck her tongue out at him, drifting, again, until he gave her another shake. "Fine, but no crying foul if I'm sound asleep by the time you get back. That was…"

"Above expectations?"

"Epic."

He wouldn't pound on his chest like some Neanderthal. He had more restraint than that. But he wanted to. Wanted to strut around the room, then yell it to the moon. How he'd somehow landed the perfect girl. Though, a tattoo with her name sounded reasonable.

"How about plan B? I text Waylen to leave some food at the door, and you can use my chest as a pillow."

God, her smile. It was more than happiness. It was love. "That sounds perfect."

Kian motioned her to wait, tugged on his pants to dash out and bring back a damp cloth. Then he spent a few minutes gently cleaning her, using it as an excuse to simply drink her in. All that smooth soft flesh just visible in the hint of moonlight filtering through the porthole.

By the time he climbed in beside her — offered her his chest — Blake looked ready to pounce on him, again. She gave his body a long slow sweep, finally settling against him when he tsked and motioned her to move in close.

She sighed against his flesh, drawing patterns along his skin. "Are you sure about this?"

"You using my chest as a pillow? Definitely."

She snorted. "Russo. This whole crazy plan to island hop or cabin hop or whatever it is Waylen thinks will eventually get Russo out in the open so you guys can do some crazy SEAL shit and take him out."

Kian stared at her, unsure how to respond. He hadn't realized she'd overheard him, Waylen and Porter talking, earlier. That Porter didn't want Russo to walk away from this still breathing.

She shook her head. "SEALs. Just remember your promise not to die on me."

"It's hard to forget when you keep reminding me. And while we're at it, you keep your ass in one piece, too."

She merely smiled, then rested her cheek against his chest. But not before he saw the way her eyes had narrowed. Or the tight press of her lips as she'd turned away. She'd obviously meant what she'd said.

That she'd make the tough call if it came down to that.

Not a problem. He'd just have to make sure it didn't. Convince her that he had her back, no matter what they faced. Was able to dive in front or tug her behind him at a moment's notice. Anything and everything to guarantee her safety.

Which explained why, four days later as they pulled into their next stop, he was still on whatever alert was above DEFCON one. They'd arrived at some secluded, off-grid area on Molokai where Waylen's friend Mano had a few rustic cabins. Nothing fancy, just enough to keep his team out of the elements — more like camping with style than actual structures. And about as deserted as they could get.

The perfect place to put an end to Russo.

The Scarab cut past them, Harlan driving with Porter taking a turn as scout. Looking far more at ease than Kian would have thought considering the water was a bit rougher today. The two men would do one more circuit, then pull in behind the main vessel. Make it look like every other place they'd stopped. Give Russo's men the green light to make their move.

And Kian's team would be waiting.

Blake finally ambled over to the railing once the other men had anchored the Scarab and joined them, gazing out at the lush forest set against the pristine blue waters. She'd been uncharacteristically quiet all day, and Kian got the sense something was brewing. That, maybe she'd figured out they were planning an ambush. Not that he'd liked keeping intel from her, but Porter had insisted that they stay on the down low until they knew for sure Russo was tailing them. Some marshal code.

Kian had resisted, but in the end, he knew it was Porter he needed to soothe so the man didn't turn and tell Blake to run, again. Because the guy would, no hesitation if he thought it was their only recourse. And Kian really didn't want to go down that route when they still had options. When his team was still Blake's best chance for a permanent solution.

She nodded at the wild landscape, mouth pinched tight, brow furrowed. "Molokai? Really?"

Kian grinned. "What's not to love? It's a tropical paradise."

"And as secluded as you can get, other than maybe Lanai. Though, that's probably up for debate." She turned to face Kian. "But it's the perfect place to stage your assault."

Kian didn't so much as allow his mouth to twitch, all the while cursing inwardly. He hated being right. "Assault?"

"Please. Do you honestly think I haven't noticed that boat tailing us for the past two days? They've been good. Have stayed mostly out of sight. But I know a gun-running vessel when I see one, and that cruiser has Russo written all over it."

Blake merely hitched out a hip when the men all exchanged a look. "Did you forget I was Coast Guard for fifteen years or did you just assume I was shit at my job?"

"Whoa. We didn't assume anything, least of all that you weren't anything but fucking amazing. We just didn't say anything because we can't be sure it's one of Russo's."

"Yeah, you can. Because no one else would be following us." She crossed her arms over her chest. "You all tote this whole team bullshit, yet, from where I'm standing, I'm the odd man out."

Porter stepped forward, cutting Kian off. "I'm the one who insisted we keep you out of the loop. Who told Kian to zip it, or I'd pull rank and spirit you out of here. You know the score, Blake. You've been through this more than any other witness I've ever had to protect. Your job is to keep your head down and out of the line of fire. Regardless of what you did before."

"Except where this is exactly what I spent the past several years with the TACLET doing. Or did that part also slip your mind?"

"You're not an officer, anymore."

"And they're not in the Navy, but you don't seem to have an issue with them playing the part of SEALs, again."

"Russo isn't looking to put a bullet between their eyes. Sure, he'll take out anyone who stands in his way, but you're the target. You know what happens if he's granted an appeal and you're not around to defend your testimony."

Blake closed the distance between them, going toe-to-toe with the marshal. "The man escaped from prison. Pretty damn sure that negates any chance at an appeal."

"Not if he owns a judge or three, and I have no doubts he does. The reason he never got the death penalty to begin with."

"All the more reason to have me help you eliminate him, then. Because that's also the plan, right? No second chances, I believe you said."

Porter groaned, running a hand through his hair. "Christ, you're a pain in my ass."

"My father didn't raise me to be a pushover. You know that better than anyone. And he didn't persuade me to forgo the Navy or the Air Force for the Coast Guard because he thought it was safer. He was afraid my talent, as he put it, would be wasted if I didn't get to do the really scary shit. So, stop pretending his blood isn't running through my veins, and keep me in the damn loop."

Raider motioned to Harlan that he'd deal with the situation, then inched forward, gently getting them to each take a step back. "I think you two need to go to neutral corners before Blake socks you in the eye, Porter."

Porter grumbled something under his breath before he turned then walked over to the railing — focused on the horizon.

Raider nodded, giving Blake an arch of his brow. "Your father is the reason you joined the Coast Guard? He must be extremely proud."

Her chin quivered for a moment. Not that the others might have noticed, but Kian did. Was so intimately in tune with her, he would know if she sneezed differently. "He was."

Raider glanced at Kian, then back to her. "He's no longer with us, then."

It hadn't been a question and Blake merely nodded. "He was killed in action five years ago."

Kian moved in beside her. "You told me flying ran in the family. Was your father a pilot?"

That got him a genuine smile. Not a happy one, but she was obviously immensely proud of her dad. "Navy pilot for damn near thirty years."

Well shit.

"I should have asked you that before, but…" But he'd been too busy falling in love — finally getting a taste of her — to ask the important questions. Something that was coming back to bite him in the ass, now. "Which reminds me. We don't even know your real name."

She looked down as she toed the deck. "Does it matter? I'm not that girl, anymore."

"Of course, it matters to them, Blake. Christ, you're fucking honorable to a fault." Porter rejoined them. "It's Carmichael. Blake Amelia Carmichael. Her father was Commander Jacob Carmichael. He was killed in a covert mission involving a joint special operational command with a SEAL team and a Ranger unit. Was the only reason those men ever made it home."

Kian closed his eyes, cursing under his breath before gazing at his buddies — acknowledging the truth mirrored in their expressions. This couldn't be happening. Out of all the missions they'd under-gone, surely fate wouldn't have orchestrated this outcome. "Shit."

Porter frowned. "What... no."

Blake snorted, drawing all their attention. But she didn't glare at them the way Kian thought she would. Hell, the way she should. Instead, that smile lifted slightly. "It was your team."

Kian looked around, again, praying one of his buddies had all the right words. Knew what to say to make this remotely okay. That her father had died saving their asses, when Blake held up her hand.

She shook her head, a few tears slipping down her cheeks. "Don't. My dad knew the risks. We all did. And he lived and died doing what he loved. The only way he wanted to go out, if I'm being honest. I think that's why he never gave it up. Passed up a bunch of promotional opportunities. Transfers that would have made him an admiral long before that. He needed to be where the action was. Saving lives."

She walked forward, palming him jaw. "I'm just glad he was there for all of you when you needed him the most. Like he always was for me."

She retreated slightly, wrapping her arms around her waist. Looking lost and determined all at the same time, and he had to force himself to hold his ground instead of marching over — taking her in his arm. "But that means you know how I was raised. And I'm not sitting this out on the sidelines. So, either you all level with me, or I take the Scarab and finish this, myself. And I will. I'm as good behind the wheel of a boat as I am in the cockpit. Damn good shot, too." She looked directly at Lane. "And not just with an M4."

Lane chuckled. "I have no doubts you could beat my ass in a competition."

She snorted. "I said good. Not exceptional. But I can definitely hold my own, which is why I'm alive and four of Russo's men, aren't."

Kian glanced at Porter, giving the man a shake of his head. "You're right. And we should have told you the moment we suspected everything, Porter's warning be damned. But I'm not ashamed to admit my heart had a hard time finding the words. I love you, Blake. That's messed with my head. Changed how I see every threat. Just the thought of you getting hurt on my watch…"

Her gaze softened, all that love shining through. "It's not just your watch. And I'm done running."

"Then, we'd best get our defenses set up before Russo's men try anything. And we're pretty sure they will. It just won't go as planned."

She nodded. "Good. Because this ends tonight."

idnight.

And still nothing.

Blake rolled her shoulders, drawing in a deep breath in an effort to ease the nervous flutter in her chest. While she was accustomed to dangerous missions, waiting for something to happen was new. And she didn't know how the men looked so relaxed when Russo's entourage could be landing on the beach, right now.

Kian nudged her thigh. "You okay?"

Of course he'd noticed she was anxious. The man seemed to have become an expert in reading her body language since they'd tumbled in the sheets four nights ago. Or maybe he'd been reading her from the start. Either way, it was as annoying as it was sweet.

She faked a smile. "Fine. Why?"

He tsked, leaning in close. "I really hope you lied better in the Coast Guard, sweetheart, because it's obvious you're uptight. Honestly, I'd be more worried if you weren't. Waiting sucks. No doubt about it."

"First of all, I lie just fine. And second, none of you seem uptight."

He shrugged. "Waiting is part of every mission. Sometimes to the point you wonder if it's ever going to happen. We've all gotten used to it. Not that it's fun, but it's part of being a SEAL. I imagine it's completely the opposite for you. You got a call and had to respond as fast as possible. Lives on the line and all that. So, this is new."

She rolled her shoulders, again, scanning the area. Lane was off in some kind of sniper nest. Blake didn't even know where, just that he'd be "watching" and providing an overwatch. Raider had set up a few perimeter countermeasures, as he'd put it. Nothing that would do any permanent damage to the delicate ecosystem. More of a sound and light show. Enough to give them a warning that shit was going down.

Harlan was just sitting and talking to Porter around the small fire they had going. Not enough to bathe the area in light. Just a small glow they hoped would draw in Russo's men.

She pursed her lips, finally meeting Kian's gaze. "What if they don't make a move?"

"They will."

"How can you be so sure? They've been following us for two days and haven't so much as fired a single shot when they could have."

"While I don't know Henry Russo, I know his type. He wants you to know he's on to you. Have you agonizing over where and when he'll attack. But I'm betting he also needs to be fairly confident we can't call in backup, and he won't get caught by the Coast Guard or even idle onlookers. He's in this mess because you saw him pulling the trigger. I can't imagine he's going to make that mistake, again. And this is his best chance at taking us out."

Blake inhaled, rerunning the last few days since they'd left. "Oh my god, you all planned this from the start, didn't you? It hasn't been some random hop from island to island. You wanted him to see us leave the Big Island and you wanted him to follow us all the way here. To limit any collateral damage."

God, the smile he flashed her. "Waylen always has a plan. Some good. Some questionable. But he always has something. This one was better than most."

"And you didn't tell me because…"

"Because you're so hellbent on sacrificing yourself to save all of us, I didn't want you diving off the boat and trying to swim here that first day. Besides, it was all contingent on Russo actually tagging along. We weren't sure he'd arrange boats and men. Guess we got lucky."

She gave him her best stink eye. "You're so getting a beat down when this is over."

"As long as you're breathing and in one piece, I'll take it."

"Oh no. Don't try to charm your way out. Just wait until we're up in the air, next. I'll get my revenge."

He took her hand and raised it to his mouth, softly kissing the back. "Deal."

"Jackass."

He smiled, then pulled her in for a long, slow kiss. The kind that had led to them making love for hours the past few nights. Not that it would end that way tonight. This was more of a distraction to ease her tension.

Until a resounding bang echoed through the forest, the beach lighting up like the Fourth of July.

Kian was on his feet with her at his side a heart-beat later, weapon already in his left hand. He made a few signals with his right, nodding at his buddies as they dispersed. Literally vanished into the trees in a matter of seconds. There, then gone. Even Porter disappeared as if he'd run covert missions for years. And hell, maybe he had. The man rarely talked about his past. Seemed to prefer people not knowing just how skilled he was. Though, thinking back to all the times he'd safeguarded her over the eighteen months she'd been in protective custody, the guy had never missed a shot.

Kian glanced at his watch, then over to her. "I know you're a trained warrior. That you can run and jump and shoot as well as any of us, but this one time…"

She smiled. "I'll stick to your ass like glue and not take any wild chances."

She didn't add the part where all bets were off if his or his buddies' lives were at stake. That she'd never be able to look at herself in the mirror with their blood on her hands. She already had enough bad memories of not getting to her teammates in time to save them. She wouldn't repeat that. Not if she wanted a future she could live with.

And she really wanted a future with Kian.

He inhaled, held it then nodded in return. "You know the plan. We try to lead whatever men my team doesn't take out over toward that other beach where we'll have a few surprises waiting. Waylen and Porter will meet us there with the Scarab. Then, it's out to Russo's main yacht where I'll have a personal chat with him."

"You mean, where U.S. Deputy Marshal Porter will arrest his ass as a wanted felon."

"Exactly what I said. You ready?"

Kian didn't wait for her to reply, just grabbed her hand then took off. He paused long enough to toss the bucket of sand over the small flames, casting the area into total darkness. Nothing but the stars and rising moon to guide their way.

Not that Kian seemed to have any trouble navigating the area. One minute in, and he had them on course to that beach — probably a quarter of the way already. He stayed low, weaving them through the trees and underbrush, following a path that barely passed as an animal trail. But he made it look easy, stopping once they reached a thick stand of trees.

He motioned for her to get behind them. "I'm going to help out the guys. Please stay here, and if anyone other than me pops out of the forest…"

"I don't need to stay hidden. I can help."

Kian moved in close, somehow still scanning the area while looking her in the eyes. "I know. And I promise, the next time crazed men are after you, I'll let you take point. But if Russo gets his hands on you…"

"This isn't just about Russo."

He clenched his jaw, making the muscle in his temple jump. "I love you, Blake."

"And I love you. Do you think I'll be remotely okay if anything happens to you?"

"I just…"

She sighed. "That flight I promised to take you on just got even rougher. And it now involves a closeup view of Kilauea in all her glory."

He smiled, dipped down for a quick kiss. "Sounds perfect. I won't be long."

He turned, gazed back at her for what seemed like forever, as if he was putting everything into memory in case he didn't get another chance. Then he vanished. Just like his buddies had. His silhouette strong and tall against the dim light one second, nothing but empty forest the next. No sound. No branches moving or twigs snapping.

Just dead space.

God, she hoped that wasn't the last time she ever saw him still breathing. That she'd have to face a future where she'd gotten the only man she knew she'd ever love killed. And that wasn't even considering the fallout if his team got hurt. What if Presley lost Waylen? Or Cassie lost Lane? And Harlan and Storm were just figuring everything out. Like Raider and Piper reconnecting. Discovering they needed to give their love another try.

Blake glanced at the gun in her hand. Kian had gotten her a Beretta, claiming it fit her hand. Would allow her to shoot one-handed if necessary. Something about planning for the worst. She was simply touched he'd thought of her and had picked the same weapon she'd had as her personal firearm throughout her career with the Coast Guard.

A reminder that it was time she remembered exactly who she was. And after three years of hiding, she was done sticking to the shadows. Which meant, making her own contingency plan if things went sideways. How she could eliminate Russo if it came down to it.

Blake moved into the best position and waited. She'd give Kian fifteen minutes, then she was going hunting.

———

Kian ducked beneath some branches, sticking to the shadows as he doubled back toward the camp. Cursing the eerie silence that enveloped the forest. Other than the initial display from Raider's counter-measures, Kian hadn't heard so much as a single gunshot. Which meant, these tangos weren't Russo's usual thugs.

It made sense, especially when the man's crew had tracked them down at Hawk's ranch. While the Brotherhood Protectors didn't advertise their company to the general public, it wasn't a secret. And Kian had no doubts Russo had the kind of connections to source out what kind of threat his people would be facing.

And that meant these men were expecting Kian's team's level of expertise and still thought they could win.

He glanced back at the path where he'd left Blake, questioning if he should alter his plans — stay by her side. While he knew she was more than capable of handling herself, if these tangos had come prepared to kill a SEAL team, it might be beyond what she'd faced in the Coast Guard. If she was in the air, he'd bet his ass that she could outsmart and outfly anyone Russo had on his payroll. But on the ground, surrounded by rainforest, in the dark…

This was his wheelhouse. And he didn't lose.

A scuff. Off to the right. Barely discernible, but he'd caught it. Knew there was some asshole trying to flank him. Whether the guy knew Kian was there or was just following the route they'd taken — how they'd bent the leaves and left more of a path through the trees than a simple animal trail — he wasn't sure. Only that the bastard was heading for Blake.

No fucking way he was leaving her to face some highly trained mercenary.

He turned, making his way along a parallel route. The guy was moving slowly, carefully picking his way through the underbrush. Trying not to make a sound.

But he wasn't silent.

Kian crept over to the asshole's side, slipping in behind him. He didn't rush, crouching low when the guy spun, checking his six for a few moments before continuing up the trail. Either a sixth sense or a routine scan of the forest. Not that it mattered.

He hadn't spotted Kian, and that would be the man's last mistake.

A jump up and a few racing steps forward, and Kian was right behind the guy — inside the strike zone. Realizing the bastard had Kevlar and NVGs only showcased he was more than the average fare — meant serious business. It also meant Kian couldn't go for a quick shot.

Not a problem. A grab and a kick, and he had the fucker's knee dislocated — the bastard's head turned off to one side. All that was left was a quick swipe of his knife and it was over. The guy's body limp on the path once Kian released him. No cries for help. No shouting. Just a slight gurgle of the asshole's last breath mixed with the flow of blood, then silence.

One down.

He dragged the man off to the side, hiding him beneath a bunch of low-hanging palm leaves, then headed back toward his buddies. While his heart wanted him to return to Blake's side, he knew he needed to trust in her skill if he had any chance of spending the rest of his life with her. Believe that she could handle the odd tango if any got past him.

He didn't plan on any getting past him.

The rising moon added a slight glow to the forest floor as he wove through the trees, fast but controlled. Just another few minutes and he'd be back at the campsite — should be able to track down Raider or Harlan.

They'd had to forgo with the usual communication tech. Porter had been concerned about Russo discovering their frequency — listening in. The marshal hadn't elaborated, but Kian felt as if the man suspected there was a mole involved. And with no cell service, they'd been left to do things the old-fashioned way.

Having Raider appear out of the brush a moment later had Kian stopping short — assessing the situation. Spying four silhouettes dressed in black racing out of the forest behind his buddy confirmed the guy he'd eliminated wasn't the only one armed for resistance. Not with them wearing the same body armor. What looked like M4s and AKs with pistols and grenades strapped to their vests.

Kian popped up enough for Raider to see him, gun ready. No worries about whether the shots would echo through the forest or not. Give away his position. Raider looked up then dove, disappearing beneath the brush.

That was all the opening Kian needed. Three head shots, three hits, with the fourth going wide. He recalculated and fired just as a bullet grazed his thigh — had him reeling back a step. But the asshole dropped a second later, his shot hitting home.

Raider moved in beside him, gun at the ready, what looked like a similar graze on his arm. "There's way more than we planned on. Close to thirty. Russo's definitely got a boat anchored somewhere just out of sight. Harlan's taken out five, alone. I was working on number six with my knife when that whole group charged me." He slapped Kian on the chest. "Thanks for the save."

"My pleasure. Your arm okay?"

"Better than your thigh."

He smiled. Raider rarely took anything seriously. "Lane still in position?"

"He's got our backs covered once we draw them to the Scarab. I saw Waylen and Porter race off. A couple boats followed, but there were only two onboard each. They'll have them eliminated in no time."

Raider arched a brow. "I swear Porter's an ex-Army Ranger. He hit one of those assholes while jumping into the boat with only a second to aim. Guy's exceptional."

"I figured as much after the hits from the back of the truck. I'll go right. You stay left. Blake's half a mile up at that stand of trees. She's armed so... don't surprise her if you reach her before me. I have a feeling she's far more skilled than my heart's willing to believe."

"She's something. Stay low. There was another group heading east when I made a run for it. Probably trying to flank the other side — come in behind her."

Kian nodded then took off, ignoring the burn along his thigh. Nothing too serious but the damn thing would scar. Not that he cared. He'd get a thousand scars to keep Blake and his buddies safe.

Branches cracked and broke behind him. Apparently, Russo's men weren't worried about stealth, anymore. Not after hearing the shots. Kian headed farther east, cutting in behind the group Raider had mentioned. They were only a few hundred meters away from Blake's position, and far too close for Kian's liking.

He ran ahead, scrambling over an outcrop of rocks, then dropping down the other side — landing just off to their left. The guy taking point turned. Gasped. Then fell a moment later. The rest scattered, firing off a flurry of bullets. They cut through the palm leaves, ricocheting off the rocks behind him. Leaving another groove across the top of his shoulder.

He hit the dirt, waited for a lull then popped up — catching one merc as he changed his magazine. A dive and a roll, and he was in close to the next — the one who'd tried to charge him. Catch him by surprise.

A jab of his knife, and the guy was down. Not quite dead, but Kian doubted he'd be getting back up. Kian switched to his Sig, dropping two more when they showed their heads around a couple trees. Gave him just enough of a target to take them out.

Another group down.

Shots sounding from Blake's direction had him racing up the path. Leaping over rocks and dodging branches. He didn't worry that he was making noise, not when that group he'd heard could have slipped past him. He doubted it with Raider manning the other side, but shit happened.

He hit the opening still running, gun sweeping the area, ready to take out anyone targeting Blake. Three men were on the ground, blood pooling beneath their bodies, a few groans suggesting they weren't all dead.

Blake spun, her weapon aimed his way before she inhaled, and lowered it, shaking her head. "Christ, I nearly fired."

He didn't slow until he'd reached her, doing his best to block any viable shot if more men jumped out of the trees. "I heard the shots..."

He didn't add that he wasn't sure what he was going to find. If she was injured. Dead.

Blake moved in behind him, guarding his six. Just like she'd promised she would. "I told you I can handle myself. Raider showed up after I'd dropped the third guy. Took off after four more who scattered."

She gave him a quick once-over. "Shit. You're hit. Twice."

"Just grazes."

"Right, which explains why there's so much blood." She muttered something under her breath, tugging on his sleeve. "Take a moment to at least slow the bleeding. I can take point."

"There'll be time to patch up wounds, later. We need to head to the rendezvous site. See if Waylen's made it there, yet. Russo must really want you. He's pulled out all the stops, this time."

"I told you he had unlimited resources. The guy's insane."

"Something tells me he wants you alive. Which was why those men at the clinic didn't shoot until we started firing. I have a feeling he wants to kill you, himself. And that's our advantage."

"Tell that to all the men out here because I'm not sure they got that memo."

Kian grinned. "They're aiming at us, sweetheart. But, no sense taking any chances. You got enough ammo?"

"Only used three shots. I'm good."

He looked over at her. "I know you're skilled, I just…"

She snorted. "You love me."

"Cliché, but true."

"Try not to take any more hits. Even a guy your

size will run out of blood. I've got your six. Lead the way."

He pulled her in for a quick kiss, then took off, again. Slower than before, checking every direction before taking his next step. He booted one of the men in the head when he looked as if he was trying to push onto his elbow, before continuing on. That eerie silence hung over the forest, the stillness making the hairs on the back of his neck prickle.

Kian stopped, crouching behind more low leaves. He hadn't spent twenty years in the service without knowing an ambush when he sensed it. And that voice inside his head was screaming there were men just waiting for him and Blake to step out of the trees and make a dash across the beach.

Blake tucked in behind him. She didn't ask why he'd stopped and was continuously scanning the area around them. He didn't know if it was simply her trust in him or that she sensed that something was off, too. Regardless, he made a mental note to thank her later. And not just for this. For not shooting him in the ass for wanting to protect her when she'd proven she was every bit the warrior he was.

They waited, that silence weighing heavily on his shoulders, when a stick cracked off to his right followed by a hushed grunt. He motioned for her to stay, creeping forward, when Raider popped up enough for Kian to spot him. He motioned for them to join him, covering their asses as Kian grabbed her hand, then darted across to Raider's position.

Another tango was at Raider's feet when they moved in behind him. His buddy motioned toward the rendezvous site. "I've cleared the path to the beach. Waylen's got the boat ready by that long stretch of rocks. You should be able to jump right in. You two go ahead. I'll set off my countermeasures when those assholes on the other side of that rock formation try to follow you onto the sand."

Blake shook her head. "We're not leaving without you."

"Harlan was just here. He's procured one of their boats and will be waiting for me by the camp. I'll hoof it back and we'll make sure any remaining forces don't have a way off the island other than swimming, then meet you at the main boat. Trust me. I'll be fine. Just like old times."

"Right, until I have to tell Piper you didn't quite make it."

"Piper knows the deal, and she'd be the first one to tear me a new one if I didn't do all I could to help you. Go. I'll see you shortly."

Blake didn't reply, but Kian knew she wasn't happy. That their little ambush had turned into a full-scale war. Though, he doubted even Porter had anticipated the sheer number of men Russo had hired. Which made Kian's idea of Russo wanting her alive a bit overzealous. Still... Kian couldn't quite shake that feeling. That if Blake hadn't been armed or was only half as good as she claimed, she'd be hogtied in the back of one of those boats, heading for Russo's yacht.

Kian slapped Raider on the back, then leaned into Blake. "I know this is hard for you, letting others take the risk, but it's almost over. We've taken out the bulk of his forces. And the rest will be marooned until the Coast Guard comes to round them up. This is the eleventh hour, sweetheart. And we're all still breathing. Time to end it."

----

15

*B*lake followed Kian out of the brush and onto the rocks, trying not to imagine all the ways she could still get his team killed. How Raider might not make it back to Harlan, or that they could both get killed if Russo had more boats. The kind with mounted machine guns or rocket launchers. Just like the one they'd salvaged off of Puerto Rico — what had gotten this whole sordid ball rolling in the first place.

She glanced at Kian's thigh, wincing at the large bloody stain on his cargo pants. The one getting bigger by the second. Graze, her ass. He probably still had the bullet lodged beneath the skin. Not that it was slowing him down. Hell, he wasn't even really limping. Just the occasional drag of that leg that was almost unnoticeable.

She'd noticed. Had spied the graze on Raider's

arm, too. That had looked disturbingly like the one Harlan had gotten during their truck race out of the ranch. All she needed was for Waylen and Lane to get hit, and she'll have gotten Kian's entire team injured.

That was the hard part. Sure, she'd gladly take a bullet for them, but knowing they'd do the same — had already gotten hit — messed with her brain. Made all of this acutely real, again, after she'd finally started to think she might be free. That time and distance had taken the fight out of Henry Russo.

She'd been wrong, and that one stupid video might be the reason these brave men didn't get the futures they'd been shaping.

Kian slowed just enough to shove her in front — block any possible hits from behind as they closed in on the edge of the rocks. Where Raider had said Waylen was waiting. She wanted to resist — tell him she should take point — but it was a wasted argument that would only eat up time they didn't have.

Having him pounce on her a moment later, taking them both to the ground, was unexpected. Hearing gunfire echo behind them a sure sign those men had followed them, just like Raider had claimed.

Kian returned a few trigger pulls before the entire beach erupted in a fountain of sand and rock, the deafening explosion vibrating through her. This was more than the lights and sounds from the first round. More like a well-placed line of C4. Or something similar. Blake didn't know if Raider had set it off manually, or if the men had activated some kind of trip wire. Either way, they were down. Nothing but blowing sand and debris visible behind them.

That was their cue to move. A jump up, and they were racing for the rocks, again, Kian still covering her. They stopped just shy of the edge, when Porter waved them on.

Kian moved in close. "You jump first. I'm right behind you."

Another decision she didn't have time to question. Not when more shots rang out behind them. Either the men had only been knocked back or there was another group. Maybe targeting Raider as he raced back to cripple the remaining boats with Harlan.

Grunting, she launched herself off, Porter catching some of her weight as she landed on the deck. Kian dropped in a second later. Another report sounded behind them, the lasting echo making her shiver.

She steadied herself as Porter released the rope they'd lassoed around one of the rocks. "Are you sure Raider will be okay? That's a lot of gunfire."

Kian grinned. "That's Lane. We'll reposition to get him on the other side of this outcrop."

All those shots had been Lane? From whatever

nest he'd been hunkered down in? She wasn't sure what shocked her more, that there were still men to eliminate or how quick the guy was reloading.

She grabbed the rail when Waylen started moving, deftly piloting the craft around a series of rocks then over to a more precarious section of cliffs. Definitely not the kind she'd want to jump from, even into the boat. With her luck, she'd break an ankle or land on one of the men.

Waylen steered toward the edge, somehow holding it remarkably steady without actually tying off. Not that there was a place he could have placed a rope, but the guy made it look easy. They'd only been waiting a couple minutes when Lane's head appeared above them. He made a few hand signals, then vanished, appearing a moment later as he leaped off the rocks, landing perfectly in the center of the boat. His rifle strapped to his back.

Kian grabbed Lane's arm to help steady him. "Not too shabby for an old man."

Lane gave him a shove. "I'm not the one Waylen nicknamed Ancient, buddy."

"Waylen's an ass."

"He is. He also isn't the one bleeding. How bad?"

Kian waved it off. "Just a couple scratches."

Lane snorted. "That's what you always say when you're the one who's hit. If it's one of us, suddenly it's a medical emergency."

"That's because you guys always go that extra mile and take a few to the important areas. Medic, remember? I'm fine. Now, how about we end this? Russo's got to be close and down on protection."

Porter motioned toward the far side of the island. "We saw a few boats coming from that direction. We figure he's hiding around the point in the next inlet. It also means he'll see us coming."

Waylen snorted. "Not when I turn off all the running lights and stick close to the shore. Don't worry, Porter. The bastard won't know what hit him until it's too late."

"SEALs." Porter looked her directly in the eyes. "I know you're not going to like this, but you need to keep your butt planted in the Scarab. I'd insist that you stay on the main vessel, but I don't need you socking me in the eye. Just keep your head down and your ass in the seat."

Blake only nodded, aware she might scream if she opened her mouth. He was right. She didn't like it, but she was the target. And the last thing they needed was for her to get in their way. She wasn't too proud to admit this was where Kian and his team excelled. She needed to give them the space to do their job without worrying she might get hurt.

But if things went for shit…

Kian gave Waylen a nod and the guy took off, once again weaving them through some nasty rocks and a section of reef before opening it up —

angling them over toward Presley's boat. The one Blake hoped was still there — still in one piece. Because it seemed viable that the mercenaries had sunk it. Or sabotaged it. Seeing it appear on the horizon looking remarkably untouched eased some of the tension in her chest. Realizing the rest of Kian's crew was already onboard, actually allowed her to gasp in some air.

Raider grabbed the rope Lane tossed them, bringing the boat alongside theirs. "We crippled all the boats we could find. There's still a chance they might have one or two hidden but for the most part, anyone still alive will be stranded until they either walk out or get caught by the authorities. And Harlan's been in contact with the Coast Guard. They're waiting for your signal, as discussed. I doubt Russo will see that one coming."

Blake snapped her gaze to Kian. "The Coast Guard's in on this?"

He grinned. "You didn't think we were going to let anyone escape, did you? And they're the authority out here. They also have skin in the game, so to speak. And when they realized they might have a chance to help Porter bring in Henry Russo?" Kian whistled. "They were all-in, sweetheart. Seems you made quite an impression over the years."

She wouldn't cry. Not yet. "I'd say it's poetic, but I'll wait until this is over. But thank you."

"Thank Porter. He's the one who thought your

fellow teammates would be the perfect backup. You ready to end this?"

She nodded, checking her supplies, again. Not that she'd gone through many, but it made the fluttering in her stomach ease. Because as prepared as they were, she knew things could still get ugly.

Lane hopped out. Apparently, he was going to be their overwatch on the main vessel along with Raider and Harlan. More backup in case Russo had any surprises left. Kian, Waylen and Porter would go aboard — eliminate any remaining forces, then grab Russo. Simple, except she knew it was anything, but.

Raider gave their boat a shove, then they were off. Slower than before. Blake wasn't sure if Waylen had checked his speed for some tactical reason, the oppressive darkness or because of an inbound storm starting to kick up the waves. Not quite at the level most captains would dock, but it had the potential to get ugly if the wind picked up. Though, that could also play to their advantage because she bet her ass Russo's guys didn't have the kind of experience her team did.

Waylen kept the boat steady, killing the lights once they got close to the peninsula lest they get spotted by any other vessels on the other side. Everything vanished into utter darkness, the moon and stars now obscured by the thick cloud layer.

God, what she wouldn't give to have her helicopter. Be able to supply support from above. That was where she had control. This... There was a reason she was a pilot and not a sailor. Sure, she could maneuver a boat better than most, but in the dark with rough seas...

Waylen didn't even blink. Kept the bow pointed where they needed to go. Even close to shore, he somehow avoided any potential pitfalls, dodging the rocks she knew lurked below. By the time they reached the edge of the cove, she was sweating. Hoping they were right, and this would all end in their favor.

Lights danced just above the surface five hundred meters off to their left, bobbing up and down with every wave. It looked like a daybridge. Obviously, Russo wasn't sparing his comfort. Not that it should surprise her. Hunting her down was nothing more than an annoyance. An inconvenience he needed to deal with before he could jet off to a country without an extradition order. Or, maybe he'd planned on staying in Florida courtesy of those judges Porter believed the man owned. Either way, the boat was large enough it could handle the waves for a bit longer before Russo might tell them leave.

Which meant this part of the mission was a go.

Porter moved in beside her, looking less impressed than previously. Though, that likely had to do with the growing waves and not the proximity of Russo's yacht. He gave her a long hard look, then moved off, grabbing the rail when the boat yawed to the left.

Kian came over, next. He didn't say anything just gave her hand a squeeze — stood lover-close to her. She glanced at his wounds, giving him a raise of her brow, but he simply smiled, and dipped in for a quick kiss.

"I'll treat them as soon as we're done. Promise. You just make sure you don't get hit if there's any crossfire."

Blake snorted. "As if I'll be taking any of the risk."

"Shit happens, sweetheart. And I need to know you're safe if I'm going to be the man you need me to be."

She tiptoed up — palmed his cheeks. "I need you to be the man that's still alive when this is done."

He smiled, kissed her, again, then turned and headed for the stern, focusing on Waylen. She couldn't tell if Waylen gave Kian some kind of hand signal or if he was just waving. Not with how dark it was. But Kian obviously understood because he signaled a few times with a flashlight back toward the other boat.

They stopped about a hundred meters off, a few men patrolling the deck clearly visible against the backlight. Blake wasn't sure why everyone was staring at the guys until one jerked then dropped. No warning, no loud report, just the waves crashing against the rocks in the distance and the guy falling out of sight.

A brief pause, then the guy at the stern vanished. Blake didn't know if he'd ducked into the cabin or jumped off the end with how quickly he'd disappeared. She rubbed her eyes, wondering if she was suffering some sort of head trauma, when the final guard at the bow fell over the front and below the surface a second later.

Lane.

Christ, that's who Kian had been signaling. And despite the constant pitching of the deck, the wind and the utter darkness, Lane had hit each man with a single shot. Sure, he'd been exceptional in the chopper, making each bullet count. But this…

This went beyond that. Put him at the top of whatever chart they used to rank snipers.

A hushed, "Hooyah," from the men, then the boat was speeding ahead. As fast as possible in the choppy waves. Waylen had them snugged against the yacht in record time — Kian tying the two together. He gave her one last look, then climbed up and over the railing, flanking to one side as Waylen took the other. Porter went last, one final glance back to ensure she wasn't following, then the men branched off, quickly disappearing from sight.

If Blake had thought waiting for Russo's men to

make a move had been agonizing, this was pure torture. Sitting there in the dark, no sounds other than the constant break of the waves against the hulls. Knowing the next few minutes would define how the rest of her life panned out.

The boat rocked hard against the yacht with the next wave, sending her sliding across the seat. She grabbed the rail, leaning over to check the ropes when a set of probes hit her shoulder, knocking her onto the deck. Pain shot through her chest, squeezing so tight she couldn't breathe. A tip of the vessel then two men were onboard, wetsuits and scuba gear making them look like monsters until they removed their masks. Hit her with the taser a second time.

Was it getting darker? Colder? She couldn't tell. Dots and streaks shifted across her vision until there were only spots of light visible. Her entire body numb from the jolts of electricity.

The bigger guy leaned over her. "Thought your bodyguards weren't ever going to leave. Russo's been waiting a long time for this. I'd hate to disappoint him, now."

16

*K*ian moved through the vessel, keeping to the shadows as much as possible. They'd cleared the upper deck and the saloon but hadn't spotted anyone else. His inner voice began yelling at him. That this was wrong. Either too easy or too quiet. And where the hell was the captain? Not that Kian had expected the man to be on the daybridge, but he should have been manning the helm adjoining the cabin. Finding it empty...

Voices echoed from the area down the set of stairs in front of them. What he assumed was Russo's stateroom. And while there was a chance the captain was in the head or talking to Russo, something felt off.

Waylen and Porter slid in beside him, nodding at the staircase. While Kian couldn't tell if Porter thought something was wrong, he knew with a single glance at Waylen that his buddy shared his concerns.

Not that they'd change their tactics, now. Better to clear the entire boat before deciding if they'd been wrong. That maybe Russo had suspected an ambush and had already left.

Kian took the stairs one at a time, careful not to make a sound. The boat pitched hard to the left for a moment, but he braced his elbow against the wall — didn't so much as move an inch. Another few steps and they were down — were clearing the head and the other stateroom, then heading for the closed door at the end. Music played in the background as someone laughed behind the closed door.

Waylen went first, showing the countdown on his hand before he turned the handle — barreled through. The guy dove across the floor, Kian going in high and right behind him with Porter bringing up their six. Scanning the room.

Realizing the voices were coming from a phone lying on the bed had his heart beating triple time. Hearing the engines from the Scarab rev, doubled it. Some insane rate that would have him stroking out. He didn't wait to explain. He simply turned and raced up the stairs, through the saloon then onto the deck. Just in time to see the boat speeding away, a tall silhouette at the helm. Another in the back.

Dead.

That's how he felt. Ice cold. Knowing that, regardless of how hard he tried, he'd never be able to catch that boat.

Waylen gave him a punch in the arm as he darted past, already working the anchor. "For god's sake, Kian, snap out of it. Porter's manning the helm. Help me get this bitch underway."

Kian pushed down the fear beading his body with sweat. One of the few times he'd ever truly been afraid. Felt as if this was it — the one mistake he wouldn't be able to fix. Taking a steadying breath, he went to work, ensuring Russo hadn't done anything crazy to the vessel before making his way to the helm. Porter already had the thing chugging forward. Not as fast as Kian would have pushed it but at least they were moving.

Porter glanced over at him, face white. Breath shallow. "They buggered the radio. But even if I could call your team or the Coast Guard, no one's reaching that Scarab before she docks wherever those assholes are taking her."

Kian didn't reply. Couldn't without shouting. He simply nodded then started flashing his light toward Lane. Praying his buddy would clue in. Though, with Blake onboard, taking a shot was risky. What if they had her propped up beside them? A physical barrier between them and any possible shot. It's what he'd do if he was in their position.

Waylen joined them on the bridge. "Not to be a prick, Porter, but…"

Porter moved out of the way. "I'm not ashamed to say you have more skill with a boat than I do. I just hope it's enough."

Waylen didn't answer, just bottomed the throttle — got that yacht rocking through the waves.

Kian placed his hand on his buddy's shoulder. He wouldn't tell his buddy not to kill them by going faster than was safe for the conditions. Not with Blake's life on the line.

He should have seen this coming. Had thought all along that Russo would want to pull the trigger himself. He should have trusted in his instincts instead of getting cocky. Thinking they could easily outsmart the other man.

Porter sighed. "I know this won't help, but it's not your fault. I've been involved in witness protection since I joined the marshals twenty years ago, and I've never come up against this kind of determination. I know my theory's right. Russo has someone involved working for him."

Kian took a breath. Reminded himself Porter wasn't to blame, either. "You thinking inside the Coast Guard?"

"Well, it's not me, and it's not your team, so you do the math. They're fucking dead by the time I'm done, though."

"Oh, they'll wish they were. I promise you that.

Russo, too, because if he puts so much as a scratch on Blake…"

Empty threats when they all knew Russo would kill her. No hesitations. No doubts. And somehow, killing the guy after the fact was empty. Because there wasn't a future without Blake in it.

He palmed Waylen's shoulder.

Waylen grunted. "I know, but I can't get any more speed out of her. I'm already in the red."

Having the waves kick up higher and the wind increase didn't help their plight, any. Though, it meant the Scarab had to slow down, too. Being half the size, it wasn't fairing nearly as well, almost capsizing on the next big swell. What might be their only hope.

"Waylen."

Waylen glanced back at Kian. "I saw it, too. If they don't slow down further, they're going to tip her. And we'll be ready. You might want to get in a position to dive overboard. Just saying." Waylen gave him a raise of his brow. "Unless it's my turn, again."

Kian shook his head. "Nope. Definitely my turn."

Porter grabbed Kian's arm as he went to dodge past. "Are you sure? I know you're a SEAL but these waves are crazy. Quickly approaching that level I commented on before."

"I don't care if this is an incoming hurricane. If there's a chance I can save Blake, I'm going in."

"I've got lights up ahead. Several hundred meters out. Bastard was hiding in the next cove. They've still got a healthy lead, but we're gaining." Waylen glanced back at him. "If they tip…"

Kian nodded. He was more than aware of all the possible scenarios, especially if her hands were tied or they'd knocked her out. She'd sink. Fast. "Just do your best to close the distance. I'll worry about the rest."

"Roger that. And Kian…" Waylen looked him dead in the eyes. "Don't fucking die on me, or I'll give you an ass kicking."

"Like you could beat me in a fight."

"Don't make me have to find out."

Kian nodded, aware there wasn't anything left to say. Either he'd get Blake back or die trying.

Damn, she hurt.

Her head, her chest — her hair. All still jumping from the taser hits. As if she was holding onto an electrical current that wouldn't stop.

Blake tried to move her head — see if they really were still tasering her — but the signals weren't getting through. Just thinking about moving had her inching her chin to the side. Puking.

It took her a few minutes to catch her breath. Roll back. Attempt to assess the situation. Not that her brain was functioning all that well. But enough to know this was it. The last few moments she'd be alive if she didn't do something. Even if Kian and Raider got both boats moving — heading her way — they'd never reach her in time. Not with how quick the Scarab was. And that was assuming they'd realized she'd been taken.

Kian would know. Would have heard the engines rev up. Most likely saw the boat speeding away. Which meant he was racing after her, right now. Maybe running on top of the damn water in an effort to save her. Either way, she knew it would kill him if he didn't make it.

Not that she was confident they'd even reach Russo's yacht when the next swell nearly toppled the Scarab. Had the bow shooting a good sixty degrees into the air before coming down hard. Spraying water all across the interior.

The sudden splash of cold helped her shake off some of the residual effects. Not quite functioning, but at least she was able to wiggle her fingers — move one leg a fraction of an inch. It wasn't much, but it felt like a freaking victory. One worthy of a gold medal.

Especially when the next wave had whoever was piloting the vessel easing back on the throttles. Slowing the boat down to a speed that might allow

Kian and his team to catch up. *If* they were already on the way.

Blake had no doubts he'd come for her. The only question was when.

Time for her contingency plan.

Of course, that plan had involved her stealing the Scarab and facing Russo, alone. With all her faculties intact. This plan revolved around her being able to move. Period. Which seemed as farfetched as Kian reaching her before they rendezvoused with Russo.

Kian had been right. The bastard obviously wanted to kill her, himself. Finish what he'd started three years ago. And what might be her only saving grace. Especially, when the rough conditions had the other men focused on the water. On not falling overboard or capsizing the boat. Assuming she was still out cold.

And she should be. After more than two hits, she should be unconscious for the next hour. And if they'd hit her in the right spot, she probably would be. But not every part of the body transmitted the shock all that well, and she'd lucked out that they hadn't thought that part through.

Or they simply didn't see her as a threat.

Which might explain why they'd only bound her hands. She hadn't realized it before. That her wrists were plastered together. Tape, she thought, though she couldn't be sure. Only that she wasn't able to pull them apart. Not like her legs. Even with everything still blurry, her head throbbing, she had enough of her senses back to tell her ankles weren't touching. And she'd use that fact to her advantage.

Blake concentrated on moving her legs. Wiggling her toes, then her feet, until she could swing them an inch side-to-side. It wasn't much, but it gave her a glimmer of hope. If she could focus long enough to kick out the bastard's legs standing beside her during the next big swell, she might have a chance.

Except when the next big one came a few seconds later, and all she managed to do was grunt — maybe sweep her heels a few inches across the floor. Nothing like the hit she'd imagined.

She kept trying, each time getting a bit closer to actually lifting her feet off the deck. Though, if she wasn't careful, the asshole she wanted to kick would clue in, and she'd be no match for him if he started focusing on her.

Was the boat slowing down more? She could have sworn she'd heard the engines spool down, again. And the deck definitely wasn't vibrating as fast as it had been. Either they were nearly at Russo's boat, or the weather had gotten even worse.

God, she hoped it was the latter. Otherwise, by the time she'd regained enough mobility to kick the asshole, it would already too late. Not that she wouldn't still try. She would. She hadn't given up that fateful day on the pier, and she wouldn't give up now. But a bit of luck wouldn't hurt.

Feeling the boat pitch left with her shoulders suggested it really was the weather. That they were hitting the largest wave, yet. Blake readied herself. Once they rocked up, they'd dip down even farther, and that's when she'd have to strike.

Had everything frozen? Just stalled with the boat halfway up the swell? Because it seemed to take forever for the Scarab to crest the wave, her body rolling right a bit in the process. Then, it was pitching hard. Dipping down. She waited until they reached the bottom, started rolling the other way before she used every ounce of strength she could muster — got a bit of a boost from the boat as it hit that next wave.

The man was already rocking partway over the edge as he gripped the rail, what looked like a rifle clasped in one hand. She aimed at the leg baring most of his weight and managed to hit him square in the knee — buckle it.

He vanished.

No shouting, no flailing. Just her knocking his knee out and him sailing over the edge.

Had his rifle clattered to the deck? Somehow not gone over the side with him? Because it looked as if it had fallen down. That he'd released it when he'd tried to catch his weight — stop himself for going overboard.

She twisted her head, that glimmer of hope burning into full-blown excitement when she realized it was definitely the rifle. The one lucky break that might get her out of this alive. Or at least allow her to take some of the remaining men with her.

Assuming she could move enough to grab it. Fire it.

A big ask when she was still recovering from that one hit. Was using all her energy just to breathe.

Knowing she probably only had a few more seconds before the guy driving would realize his buddy wasn't in the boat got her laser focused. Grunting through the effort to wiggle over — grab the stock.

The weapon felt oddly heavy. As if they'd weighed it down. But she managed to wrap her joined hands around the grip — drag it closer.

The guy was talking on the radio. At least, that's what she thought. Mumbled words rising above the sounds of the waves. Which meant they were getting close. That he'd surely turn around to take stock any moment.

One last burst of willpower, and she had that rifle on her chest — got her body upright and leaning against the edge. A check to see if the safety was still on, then she was doing her best to point it at the driver. She wasn't sure if it was remotely in the right direction, but if she kept firing, she might get lucky and hit him.

Having the asshole turn and look her dead in the eyes a second later was all she needed to test that theory. His eyes bulged as he went for his weapon, but she was already pressing the trigger. Slamming her body into the side as the rifle went off, practically vibrating out of her hands as she swept it left to right — caught the asshole several times in the process.

He jerked then fell back over the wheel, turning the boat to the left as the engines kicked up — propelling them forward. Hitting the next wave at some odd angle that nearly capsized them.

The radio hissed, some voice yelling a name. She couldn't quite get her brain focused enough to make sense of the words, but the voice had sounded agitated. Nervous even.

Another spray of water as the Scarab dipped low lifted a bit more of the fog. Allowed her to blink enough to realize they were nearly at Russo's yacht. Lights bobbed off the bow, no more than fifty meters away. What was a collision course if she didn't stop the Scarab in time.

She couldn't. Even if she managed to stand, she'd never cover the short distance between the stern and the wheel before they crashed. Not with how drained she felt.

Of course, the collision might be the second lucky break because there wasn't any way Russo's men could avoid it, either. Get that huge yacht moving fast enough to prevent the hit.

That singular thought — that she might actually take the bastard out — gave her the last boost of strength she needed. Two seconds flat, and she was on her feet. Shaking and barely standing but upright. Another, and she was at the railing, just like the guy she'd knocked overboard.

Shouts rose from the boat, the pop of gunfire sounding around her. They were only maybe twenty meters apart now, well within striking distance. Blake braced herself in the corner, gathering her energy for one last move. What it would take to launch herself over the edge. She wouldn't survive, but it beat dying in a fiery blaze.

She took a breath, when something hit her shoulder, knocked her back. There was a moment of hang time, the water dipping down as the boat hit the next big swell, shooting up and away from her. Then she was plunging beneath the surface — everything fading into black as the ocean enveloped her, dragging her down.

17

*A*gony.

That's what this was. Following the Scarab as it got incrementally closer but knowing they wouldn't catch it before it reached Russo's yacht was nothing short of gutting. And there wasn't a damn thing Kian could do but stand there.

Seeing the boat pitch up and down, wondering if it would simply capsize with the next huge wave felt like a non-stop heart attack. He'd actually shouted out her name when the Scarab had bounced up at some ridiculous angle then plunged forward, spraying a gallon of water over the deck. The asshole piloting the boat had somehow managed not to sink it on the spot, but it had been close.

The guy had slowed down even more after that. Had obviously realized he wasn't going to make it to

Russo's vessel in one piece if he didn't take the increased bad weather into account. But even with the reduction in speed, they wouldn't catch the thing.

Waylen was pushing their yacht as hard as he could. Probably doing permanent damage to the engines. Not that Kian cared. All that mattered was that they were gaining. Painfully slowly, but still gaining.

Had the guy in the back just toppled overboard?

Kian blinked, then inhaled. No doubt about it, the asshole was gone. Just disappeared in that last huge swell. As if he'd completely lost his balanced. Or had someone give him a shove.

Blake. It had to be.

Which meant she was still alive. Still able to be saved. He started deep breathing. Expanding his lungs as much as possible to take in more air because he knew this would end in some kind of desperate water rescue. Whether it was a weird link to Blake or just one of those eerie premonitions that happened in the heat of battle, he knew he'd have to go in the water after her.

He saw Russo's other vessel more clearly, now. A huge yacht that made this one seem small. One of those mega ones that celebrities rented, only this one was probably the result of blood money. All those drugs and weapons he'd sold for profit. It bobbed in the water a few hundred meters ahead, the lights casting dots across the angry waves.

The Scarab slowed, again, as it closed in on the boat, silhouettes moving along the deck. Armed. Ready. Not that Kian could see what kind of weapons they were packing, but it was some type of rifle, the long barrel visible in the backlight. Porter was already taking up position near the front. Probably hoping to down a few of them before they could grab Blake. Assuming Waylen could get them close enough.

Not that it mattered when the driver turned a moment later, then jerked as gunfire sounded above the storm. Not loud, like it should have been, but there had been a distinctive popping sound before the guy shuddered then fell. Slumping over the wheel in the process.

The boat yawed left as it sped up, crashing through the next wave as it rushed toward the yacht. A damn collision in the making. The men on the deck started racing along the railing, waving at the boat, before shouldering their weapons.

A lone figure rose near the stern. Shaky. Noticeably smaller. Her hair whipping in the wind. She shuffled to the edge, looking as if she was going to jump when her body jerked backwards, and she tumbled over the edge, quickly disappearing beneath the waves.

"Waylen!"

Waylen angled the boat toward the impact zone, somehow getting a bit more speed out of her. Kian kept his gaze glued to where Blake had vanished, counting off each second in his head. If she was still conscious, she'd last a good minute underwater. Maybe two with her training. If she'd been knocked out…

Not that it mattered when the Scarab rammed into the yacht, exploding on impact. Sending a massive fireball fifty feet in the air. Wood and fibre-glass showered down across the water as smoke mixed with the howling wind.

Waylen danced the yacht through the debris, getting close enough Kian dove off the side — started swimming through the waves. Blake bobbed to the surface, looking as if she gulped in a lungful of air before the next wave bowled her over — dragged her back down.

He kept working, fighting the current as it tried to pull him backwards — increase the distance. Not happening. Not when he knew she wouldn't last much longer. What had looked like a bullet strike before she'd fallen overboard.

Thirty seconds, and he'd only covered half the distance — was barely making headway. Another twenty, and she breached the surface, again. Raising bound hands out of the water for a few moments before sinking, again. One huge wave cresting over her, what looked like a chunk of wood hitting her in the head.

He dove beneath the surface, covering the last of the distance underwater. Searching for any sign of her. Pieces of both boats churned with the tide, crashing into his ribs as another caught his thigh. He went deeper, trying to avoid the roll of the waves and the crushing debris, when a flash of white caught his attention.

He veered toward it, pushing harder when he recognized her hoodie. What looked like limp arms floating amidst the dark current. She didn't move when he grabbed her around the waist, kicking to take them both to the surface. Water sprayed across his face as he sucked in a breath, already towing her toward the boat.

Waylen pulled up alongside a minute later, Porter reaching over to help lift her onto the deck. Kian dropped in a moment later, rolling her to her back as he checked her vitals.

No pulse.

No breaths.

He got her into position then started compressions, nodding at Porter to give her two breaths after he'd finished thirty. Restarting when she didn't respond.

Porter paled, glancing up at him. "Kian…"

"She wasn't under that long. Still lots of time. Don't fucking quit on me now, Porter."

"I'm not… Just tell me when to breathe, again."

Kian kept working. "Now."

Nothing.

"Come on, sweetheart. Don't let that bastard win." He reached the end when she coughed, spitting out water as she tried to gulp in air. He turned her, waiting until she'd emptied most of it onto the deck before propping her against a few lifejackets. Because despite being back, she wasn't close to fine. Not with an obvious gunshot wound, a likely concussion, and what looked like burn marks on her other shoulder. Most likely from a taser.

He yanked his shirt over his head, balling it up then pressing it against the wound. She cursed, eyes rolling slightly as she started to drift off.

"Stay with me, Blake. I want to see those gorgeous baby blues."

Her eyelids fluttered, remaining half-open as she stared at him through a curtain of lashes. "Glad I stayed on the boat where it was safer."

He laughed. He couldn't help it because despite everything, she was still sane. Still his.

"Me, too. Those other marks from a taser?"

She nodded. Or at least, she tried. Barely moved her head, but he got the message. "Fuckers were waiting underwater. What happened to the Scarab?"

"It didn't make it. Took out Russo's luxury yacht in the process. Looks like you won."

"Never thought winning would hurt so much. I…"

She drifted, again, barely rousing when he rubbed her sternum. Hard.

Kian looked over his shoulder at Waylen. "I need my damn medic bag."

Waylen nodded. "Two minutes. Raider's on the way."

Two minutes. Which was a hundred and nineteen seconds longer than it should have been. And enough time she could slip into a coma. Maybe bleed out if the damn bullet had struck a major organ.

Kian put more pressure on the wound as Raider pulled the other boat up alongside. Lane jumped out, carrying his bag, before dropping it beside Kian. He had it open and was handing Kian a saline bag and some Quick Clot inside of another sixty seconds.

Lane leaned over. "Coast Guard's five minutes out."

Kian nodded. "She needs blood. Porter, any idea what type she is?"

Porter shook his head. "Sorry. It never came up."

"Figured as much, but it was worth asking. Lane, take over for Waylen. Let him know he's my first donor."

Lane took off, only to have Waylen drop down beside Kian a moment later.

His best friend shook his head. "Let me guess. You have no idea what blood type she is."

"Guess it's your lucky day."

"The curse of being a universal donor."

"It's either you or me, buddy. Unless you want to be the one to set up the direct transfusion."

Waylen rolled up his sleeve. "I'll just bleed for you."

"Thought you'd see it that way."

Porter glanced off to the left. "Coast Guard's nearly here. We can transfer over to their vessel. Should be easier for you to treat her. We'll head for Molokai's general hospital. They can airlift her if it's necessary."

Kian merely nodded, blinking when the scenery shifted. The accumulated blood loss starting to take a toll. Not that he'd pass out before he'd gotten her stable. He could die later. When it was convenient.

Lasting until they walked through the hospital doors was one of Kian's shining achievements. Having Waylen catch him before he face-planted onto the floor, one hell of a lucky break. Waylen muttered something about Kian being too stubborn for his own good, but all he heard were the doctors rattling off Blake's vitals. One of them yelling for more blood. There was a flurry of activity — doctors and nurses pouring into the room — then they were rushing her off. Talking about X-rays and whether they'd have to transfer her once the storm passed.

Porter came up alongside — gave Kian's arm a squeeze. "I won't leave her side. You have my word. You focus on not dying because she'll have my balls if she wakes up and you're not the first face she sees."

Kian snorted. "Just, keep her safe. Until I see Russo's body, I won't trust this is over."

"That might be hard. Storm took most of the bodies away. We might never know for sure."

"We'll know because if the bastard isn't dead, he'll come for her. And I'll be waiting if he does."

Porter chuckled. "Right. The guy about to bleed out is going to be waiting for the mafia kingpin. How about you worry about breathing, and I'll worry about doing my job. And if by some wild chance Henry Russo is still alive, he'll be dead before he steps one foot into her room."

"I'll hold you to that. And I'd hate to have to kill you if she gets hurt on your watch."

"Glad to know I mean enough to you it might actually pain you to pull the trigger, Fox. Rest. I'll keep your team updated."

Kian relaxed back, finding enough energy to nod at Raider. His buddy rolled his eyes but took off after Porter. Not so obvious the marshal might realize Kian had sent a teammate as backup, but enough Kian wouldn't worry. Not that Porter wasn't badass enough. Kian simply felt more at ease knowing two top-notch warriors were watching her. Would keep her safe while he couldn't.

Waylen stopped at his side, giving him a long, slow once-over. "For a medic, you really know how to fuck yourself up. Did you seriously get some of that from when you were underwater?"

"Shut up."

"Porter's right, ya know. No way we'll ever know. Which means, you might need to stay at her side permanently."

"Smart ass. Like I wasn't already planning on that."

"Then, you better let them treat you because you look like a fucking ghost."

He wanted to say he didn't care. That Blake's safety was all that mattered. How the doctors needed to focus on her, first. But the words wouldn't form on his tongue. Everything around him growing dimmer.

He thought Waylen called for one of the nurses, but all he heard was the echoed beat of Blake's heart on the monitor as he slowly closed his eyes.

Kian came back around what could have been minutes, hours, or even days later. Though, a glance at one of the windows suggested it was still dark outside. Not even a hint of daylight. He had blood and saline drips in his arm, bandages on his shoulder and thigh. Not that he could see all of them, but he felt the tug of the tape when he tried to move — had pain shooting through his chest simply shuffling an inch.

He'd definitely bruised some ribs when he'd gotten hit with that debris. But pain meant being alive, so he'd take it.

He stared at the ceiling for a while, drifting in and out when that eerie quiet he'd encountered in the forest settled over the room, not even a ticking clock or a monitor beeping in the background.

Obviously, they weren't concerned he was going to drop dead. Though, it made sense. His injuries hadn't been severe, and if he'd treated the blood loss like Blake had suggested, he wouldn't have ended up on the gurney to begin with.

Her name had him bolting upright. Ignoring the pull of stitches and the way his chest squeezed tight, making his next breath nothing more than a choppy gasp. Was Porter still watching her? Had something bad happened? What might explain why he was alone. That maybe his buddies had needed to provide backup.

He flung back the sheets, rolling his eyes at the stupid hospital gown covering his body. That damn opening probably baring his ass. But he could worry about modesty later. Once he was sure this wasn't another emergency in the making.

It took a few tries to swing his legs over the edge

— sit up. But after gaining some momentum, he managed to scoot his ass to the edge — touch the floor. The fact he was barefoot didn't help, either. Opened up the possibility of more injuries if he wasn't careful. And based on how shaky he was, avoiding obstacles would be more luck than skill.

It didn't stop him from shoving off the bed. Taking a few stumbling steps when his muscles didn't work right. Nearly dropped him to the ground. Leaning on the IV pole helped. A good reason not to yank the lines out quite yet. Using that pole as a brace got him across the floor and over to the door. He peeked out, then slowly opened it.

Nothing.

No teammates, no nurses. Not so much as a janitor mopping the floors.

That didn't bode well.

Got him running through a bunch of scenarios, none of them good. What if Russo had managed to get off the boat before the explosion? If he really had someone — or a few someones — loyal to him from within the Coast Guard, they could have snuck him onto the vessel during the rescue attempt. When the boat had been searching for survivors. Leaving Russo to make his way to the hospital once everything had quieted.

Kian scanned each direction then struck off. It wasn't fast and it wasn't pretty, but he got his feet moving. Was able to drag his ass down the corridor.

His first choice led to the staff parking lot. The next, a storeroom. By the time he was working on his third, he was exhausted. Had to stop every several steps just to breathe — find the energy to keep moving.

He definitely should have taken a moment to stem the bleeding when it started. But at the time, Blake's safety had been more important. Was still more important.

A mental pep talk, and he was walking, again. Bearing some of his weight on that damn pole, despite the fact it teetered back and forth. What he suspected was a loose nut holding on the base. The one with the wheel that occasionally clattered against the floor like those crappy shopping carts. He gave the thing a shake — got all the castors working — when the hairs prickled on the back of his neck.

He wasn't ignoring his instincts, again. Not when he'd been right all along about Russo. And this felt like another full-blown premonition. The reason he'd woken when he had. That link to Blake like when he'd known he'd have to go in the water after her. Only this was darker. More sinister. Like when he'd been heading for an ambush in the field. Every hair standing on end. The muscles in his gut tightening.

He paused at the next junction, hoping that link would direct him. It sounded crazy, but he didn't care. Not when he'd had an instant connection to her from the start. Why he'd jumped so far, so fast.

A scuff.

Off to the left.

Not much. Probably just a shoe catching a lip in a doorway, but he headed that way. Scanning each tiny window in every door that he passed. He reached another corridor then turned right when hinges creaked in the distance.

Adrenaline started kicking in. Had him moving faster. Steadier. He hit the next intersection at a decent pace, barely resting any weight on that pole. A shadow disappearing around the bend off to his right had him laser focused. He followed behind, stopping at the corner before peeking around. Blinking a few times to ensure he wasn't dreaming. Imagining the entire scene. Because he swore Henry fucking Russo was standing at the door two down on his left. Hand resting on the handle before he turned it — disappeared inside.

Kian should call for help. Pull the fire alarm. Something to get his buddies searching for him because he had nothing. Not weapons, no backup. Hell, no clothes other than that flimsy gown. The one with his ass hanging out the back.

So, moving ahead wasn't his wisest decision. But he couldn't chance the bastard would find a way to escape in all the confusion. What would have the entire hospital trying to evacuate if he pulled the fire alarm. And Kian knew if Russo got away this time, he'd disappear. Be that shadow hanging over Blake for the rest of her life.

Kian stopped at the door, taking a quick peek through the window. Some kind of locker room. Which made sense. If Russo wanted to blend in, he needed scrubs. Not to mention he might luck out and find an ID tag that had been left in one of the lockers.

Kian took a moment to slip the lines out of his arm before flipping over the pole, praying he'd been right about the nut. Seeing it halfway off was the lucky break he needed to have any chance at coming out of this alive.

It only took a few twists before the base fell into his hand. He removed the holder and bags on the top, giving the stainless steel pole a twirl for good measure, then moved back to the door. A couple deep breaths, then he was easing the door open, grinning when it didn't make a sound. The room was dark, only the faint glow of some form of light filtering in through a distant set of windows.

He darted to the right, sticking to the shadows. He didn't think there was another exit, which meant Russo was inside. With Kian. And the bastard wasn't leaving unless Kian was either unconscious or dead.

A squeak had Kian zoning in on the guy.

Heading for the locker sets over in the far corner, hoping that stupid pole would be enough.

A few more steps, and he was at the end of the row — had Russo's silhouette in view. The asshole had his back to him, too busy rooting around in a locker to notice. Not that it gave Kian much of an advantage when he spied a gun tucked into the back of the man's pants. A fucking game changer. All it would take was Henry sensing his presence, and he could fire before Kian got off a single swing of his pole.

He could double back. Pull that alarm. True, he hadn't noticed one, but there had to be one close by. Maybe in the room.

Having Russo turn as he slipped on a lab coat and clipped an ID onto the front had Kian moving. Sliding over to that first row. If he could reach the edge of the lockers before Russo, he might be able to surprise the man as he made a beeline for the door.

It only took Kian several seconds to backtrack — ready himself at the end of the first row of lockers. A cock of the pole, and he was primed, listening to the slight scuff of Russo's feet across the floor. Just enough to broadcast his progression through the room.

Kian waited until the man was practically abreast of him before stepping out — swinging that pole like a bat. He hit Russo in the arm, knocking something out of his hand as the man reeled backwards, crashing into another set of lockers. Kian moved with him, hitting him, again, once he'd recovered enough to orient himself — get that pole in the right position.

He caught the fucker in the chest, this time, doubling him over as he tumbled onto a bench. Russo clawed at the surface, regaining his balance quicker than Kian had hoped. But it didn't matter. Kian was in the zone, Blake's bruised and bloody body wavering in the back of his mind. No way he was stopping until Russo wasn't a threat.

Russo managed to get his hands in front of him, partially deflect the next blow. But it connected hard enough to tip him off the seat and onto the floor. Kian rounded the bench, his next swing knocking the gun out of Russo's hand. It clattered along the floor and under the next locker. The stroke of luck Kian needed. Especially, when his knee buckled on his subsequent step, and he crashed into the metal doors.

He gave his head a shake, poking Russo in the gut with the end of the pole when the guy lunged at him — landed a punch to his ribs before the end connected. The hit dropped the guy. Not quite out cold, but he was groaning. Barely moving.

Another stroke of luck because Kian was sliding down the locker as both legs gave out. His ass smacking the floor next to Russo. He kept that pole at the ready, each breath sending jolts of pain through his chest, as the doors burst open, Porter, Waylen and Lane busting through.

Lights flickered to life, temporarily blinding him before the men were there, grabbing Russo — cuffing the man's hands behind his back.

Porter leaned over him, mouth pinched tight. Eyes narrowed. "For the love of god, Fox, what the hell were you thinking? How the fuck did you even get out of bed? And why aren't you wearing any pants?"

Kian snorted, nearly blacked out, before blinking Porter into focus. "I…"

That's all he got out. One word.

Porter yelled something he couldn't make out, the scenery fading, again, like it had earlier.

"We had it all set up. I had a feeling that fucker hadn't died in the explosion, so we made a corridor. Had Blake's room staked out. All the nurses and doctors moved out of this wing so Russo could corner himself. Then, Waylen realizes you're not in your damn room, and all hell breaks loose. Didn't you think it was strange you hadn't run into a single freaking nurse?"

Kian shrugged. At least, he thought he did. "Blake…"

Another one-word answer, and this one drained him even more.

Porter sighed, moving off to one side when a

couple doctors appeared. "You're insane. Completely reckless. But, we've got him. And I'll be personally flying his ass back. On a private freaking jet. Now, let them get you back to bed before I have to tell Blake you're even worse off than she is."

Kian wanted to ask how she was. Tell them to just take him to her room, but he could barely keep his eyes open. Waylen moved in beside him as they shoved his ass in wheelchair — started pushing him down the hallways. He said something about him being as nuts as Blake. That they were the perfect match, but it got lost to the darkness. To the squeak of the wheels against the floor as he closed his eyes, content that he could rest for a few minutes without worrying she'd get hurt. But this was far from over, and he had no plans of letting his guard down for the foreseeable future.

18

*D*ead. Surely she was dead.

That, or this was hell. Because heaven wouldn't hurt this much. Be this cold.

Blake blinked open her eyes, cursed at the jolt of pain through her head, then closed them again. Nothing that simple should be that painful. Like breathing. All she did was suck in a small breath, and her ribs felt as if they were being pried apart. Sharp, stabbing jabs down each side, pulling her under.

She let go, floating in that numbing darkness, drifting in and out, until a steady beep pulled her back up. This time, the room didn't flip flop when she opened her eyes, the bright light making her squint.

Either it was daylight, or someone had a spotlight on her.

God, she hoped it was the first because the other meant she'd only dreamt she'd escaped. That somewhere between them tasering her and what she'd thought was her plunging into the ocean, had really been them dragging her onto Russo's boat. That when she finally focused on her surroundings, the bastard would be there. Grinning.

A shift of her head assured her she wasn't on a boat. It looked like a hospital room, complete with monitors sounding in the background and a stuffed bear sitting on a tray beside her.

She tried to push up onto her elbows — failing when the simple motion stole her next breath. Leaving her lying there, cursing.

Someone sighed from the other side of the bed, the familiar tone soothing the anxious roil of her stomach. "Out for days, and you wake up ready to fight. You are every inch the spitfire Hawk claimed the night we met."

Blake inhaled, swore against the sharp pain streaking through her ribs, then turned, looking up into the bluest eyes she'd ever seen. He had bruises over half his face and bandages peeking out through the top of his shirt.

He'd never looked more handsome.

She tried to roll her eyes, but probably only succeeded in winking at him. "Says the guy who looks like he went ten rounds with a tank and lost."

Kian moved in close, slipping her hand into his.

"At least I'm standing, sweetheart. Which is more than you'll be doing for a few days."

He leaned down, brushing his lips across her forehead. "Don't ever scare me like that, again. When you tipped over the edge and into the ocean…"

"I knew you'd come for me." She licked her lips, accepting the water he offered her. "Russo?"

"Alive, but Porter took his ass back to jail. Got him transferred to Leavenworth. He won't be bothering you for twenty to life."

She nodded, but it fell flat. Alive meant threat, and he obviously knew it, too, because he sighed, again. Brushing his thumb across the back of her hand.

Kian nodded. "I know, but… let's celebrate the win, even if it's just for now. Okay? Besides, I have a few connections in Leavenworth. Might have already had someone pay Russo a visit. If the man wants to die of old age, he'll leave you alone."

"You threatened Russo? In prison?"

"Anything for you, sweetheart."

God, the way the endearment slipped off his tongue. It made her acutely aware that, despite everything Kian and his team had done — the fighting, the extreme maneuvers — Porter would still want to move her. Put her someplace Russo didn't know about. Not that she wanted to go, but just looking at Kian's injuries brought it all into focus. That she couldn't risk everyone's life just for her own happiness.

Kian frowned, running his fingers along her cheek. "Whoa, Blake, what's wrong? You don't have to cry, sweetheart, everything's—"

"But Porter…"

She couldn't finish that statement. That Porter would tear her away from what had become her home. What was Kian's home with his team.

Kian brushed some of her hair back, his fingers lingering against her skin. So warm. So full of life. "Porter's not the enemy. He only wants what's best for you. Though, he realizes that if you're not safe here, with me and my team, then you're not safe anywhere. He did, however, suggest you change your name again."

She frowned. Had Kian implied Porter was going to recommend she stay on the Big Island? Just change her name? "Another identity?"

"Not exactly. Just a new last name. I told him I agreed, on one condition." He smiled. "That I get to pick it. How do you feel about Blake Amelia Fox?"

Blake blinked, opened her mouth, then closed it. Wanting to ask if he was serious, but unable to get anything out, because… damn. Had she heard him right?

It took her a minute to get her tongue working — do more than gasp. "Fox?"

His smile widened. Made all that light shining in through the window seem dull in comparison. "I know, it's not as cool as Garrett, but... I have to admit. I love the sound of it. Just like I love you. So, what do you say? One last change, because this one's gonna be forever."

She was crying. She knew she was. Tears slipping down her face, as she tried not to laugh — what might pull out stitches or send her into the ICU. Something to take her away from him. "Not as cool as Garrett. But I love it way more. Just like you."

Kian rolled his eyes. "You do know how this works, right? I ask you to marry me. And you say, yes, not some coded, cryptic answer."

She laughed, regretting it just like she'd imagined. "You know it hurts when I laugh."

"Then say, yes, and I'll let you go back to sleep."

"No sleeping. But yes, I'll marry you. As long as you promise you won't nearly die on me, again. And yeah, I can tell by looking at you that you came close."

"I can't let you upstage me, sweetheart. What will my teammates think if you're the only one always pushing the limits?"

"That we're a perfect fit?"

He chuckled. "Always an answer. Rest. I'll be here until I can wheel you out of here. Then, we'll find a place to call home, because I'm not living above your damn hanger."

"Deal. Now, aren't you supposed to kiss the bride?"

"Hell, yeah."

He claimed her mouth. Not long and hard. Just a soft press of his lips on hers. A promise of what was to come.

Blake hummed, resting her head against him when he climbed onto the bed. Not enough he'd hurt her, just a comforting weight next to her. He drew his fingers through her hair, lulling her back to sleep. Only this time, she didn't have to worry about nightmares or monsters. He'd be there to slay them, exactly like he'd promised.

Two weeks later…

Blake leaned against Kian as he piloted their new boat along the coast, enjoying the warm breeze blowing in off the ocean. Seagulls cried overhead, the light scent of the water filling the air. The sun was already heading toward the horizon, the first hints of orange and red painting the sky.

Everyone was on deck, music playing in the

background as they headed for the cove not far from the marina. Just enough to make everything official.

Porter ambled up beside them, beer in one hand, a piece of pizza in the other. "You know, Blake, when Kian told me he wanted you to take his last name, I thought he was dreaming. Who knew you were such a romantic."

Blake looked up at Kian, loving the way he rolled his eyes at Porter. "Guess I finally found a reason to hope, again."

Porter gagged, shaking his head at them. "Just… stop."

Kian chuckled. "Jealousy does *not* suit you, brother."

Porter paused, looking at Kian for a moment before laughing. "I just want to enjoy the win without you two making me sick. Not often I get to see the happy ending."

Kian muttered something under his breath about Porter being the romantic one, but Blake didn't miss the fact he'd called Porter, brother. That ever since the man had put his life on the line for her, Kian had made him an official member of their team. Porter had even put in for a transfer to the Honolulu office and was scheduled to start next week. While it wasn't as close as having him stationed on the Big Island with them, it was a quick chopper ride, and Blake had already promised to make a weekly trip so Porter could hang with the rest of the team.

Waylen walked over and handed Porter another beer. "Just keep drinking, buddy. They get less nauseating the drunker you are."

Kian gave Waylen a shove. "Says the guy who just spent the last ten minutes making out with his knocked-up girlfriend. At least Blake and I are getting the order right."

"Really? Has she taken a pregnancy test, then? Because I won't believe it until I see it."

Blake glared at the men. "I'm not pregnant. And no, I'm not going to pee on a stick just to prove it. *If* it happens, and that's a big if, I'm sure you'll be the first to know. And there's no order, but Kian's right. You two are worse than us."

"We'll have to agree to disagree." Waylen looked around. "This looks like a pretty great spot. And if I have to listen to Harlan practice all the vow shit one more time, I'm going to toss his ass off the boat and you two will have to make a trip to the courthouse."

Kian laughed. "Hey, he was the only one who volunteered to get ordained."

"Like any of us had a choice. It was always going to be him."

Kian simply grinned, slowing the boat until it was gently bobbing on the easy waves. Nothing like the night she'd nearly died. What seemed like a life-time ago.

Presley met her by the bow, handing her some flowers. They hadn't bothered with anything fancy. Just their friends, food, drinks and the sun setting the scene. Blake had opted for a simple blue dress to match Kian's button up and shorts. Like the white one he'd worn that first night, only without the blood. His buddies were just as casual, and all the ladies wore skirts.

Harlan looked oddly relaxed as he started the ceremony, getting everything right. Which is what Blake had expected. The man didn't do anything half-assed.

One long soul-searing kiss, and it was done. Except for the part where his buddies started blowing freaking bubbles at them. What Blake suspected had been Presley's doing. Though, seeing Presley catch the bouquet when Blake all but launched it at her face was enough payback.

There was shouting and singing, the boat rocking as they partied until Waylen finally took the helm — started the short ride back to the marina.

Blake smiled as Kian tugged her against his chest, leaning against the rail — watching their friends gather on the deck, still talking. "They look happy."

Kian kissed her neck, grinning against her skin. "Almost as happy a me."

"Charmer."

"Gotta keep you coming back for more, sweetheart."

"You already promised me this was the last time I'd have to change my name. I'm holding you to that." She glanced back at him. "And yes, that was both a reminder and a threat."

He laughed. "I'm still waiting on that flight around an erupting volcano you promised me. I won't press my luck."

"Oh, it's coming." She leaned against him, enjoying the simple pleasure of being in his arms. "Thank you."

"For what?"

"Everything. Not letting me run off when you had the chance. Pulling me out of the ocean. Beating Russo up with a damn IV pole. But mostly for giving me back my life."

"It's still not your old one."

"It's better because I have you." She turned in his arms, wrapping hers around his neck. "Though, I don't remember agreeing to the name of our boat."

His smile made the sunset look black and white. "I definitely asked you."

"Asking me while I was hopped out on meds doesn't count."

"You're just sore because I didn't name it squid."

"Oh, and Puddle Pirate is better? I thought I'd

have to take Presley to the clinic. She laughed so hard, she gave herself cramps."

"At least I didn't name it Kian. Or Blake."

She coughed, then laughed. "Damn, I love you."

"Good. Because I got Porter to make up all the official documents, and the guy will have my balls if you suddenly change your mind."

"Already said, 'I do,' sailor. You're stuck with me, now."

"Then, shut up and kiss me, already, puddle pirate."

"That's Mrs. Puddle Pirate to you, squid."

"Hell yeah, it is."

EPILOGUE

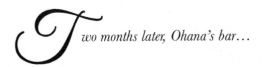 *wo months later, Ohana's bar…*

Kian stood behind the bar, cracking open another beer before handing it to one of the servers. She thanked him then strode off, laughing with the group of tourists sitting on the far side. Waylen was rocking the place with a pretty impressive version of a classic Bob Seger song on the piano, with Presley adding some harmonics. Harlan and Raider were sitting with Storm and Piper at another table, tapping along to the music as they laughed at something one of them had said.

All it all, it was a perfect grand re-opening night for Ohana's bar.

Kian shook his head. He still couldn't believe

they'd bought the place. Sure, they all loved unwinding here after working for the Brotherhood Protectors — a gig that kept them far busier than Kian could have predicted — but buying the bar had been special. Their own little slice of paradise that guaranteed to keep the team together, no matter how their lives changed.

Which still shocked him. How they'd all found someone special from that unscheduled eruption. Not that he'd embraced that part of living on the Big Island. But seeing how it had brought Blake into his life, he was learning to make peace with the constant threat of fire-breathing mountains.

The door opened as Blake swept into the bar, her helmet under one arm, a folder under the other. After living in the loft apartment in her hanger, they'd finally found a quaint little cottage to call home, and she'd stopped to pick up the paperwork after her last flight.

A shiver wove down his back, but he shook it off. Despite having a couple of badass guards give Russo a few intense warnings not to mess with her, Kian still didn't feel at ease when she was on her own. Which wasn't often. Between him and his team, they found a way to ensure she always had backup. Hawk's guys pitched in, too.

And of course, U.S. Deputy Marshal Adam Porter had become a regular visitor — hell, part of the family — spending most of his free time on the

Big Island. Having a chopper at his disposal hadn't hurt any, but Kian had an inkling the man would have found a way over, regardless.

He was definitely one of the good guys. Had made it his mission to source out who had been helping Russo track Blake. And while he hadn't made any arrests, yet, he'd told Kian he was close.

Blake smiled as she stopped to say hello to his teammates before heading for the bar. She rolled her eyes at Lane and Cassie kissing off to one side, sliding into the seat in front of him. Kian leaned over — tugged her in for a long, wet kiss.

She stayed half-bent over the counter, looking him in the eyes as if he was the answer to the mystery of life, before finally sitting back down. "If I'd known you were going to kiss me like that, I would have gone straight to the back so you could pin me to the wall."

He coughed, groaning against the sudden tightening in his pants, before shaking his head. "You said that on purpose."

"Maybe. But I promise to help you out as soon as you take me home. Speaking of which… it's official. As of next week, we no longer have to live with the smell of jet fuel and oil cans."

"As hard as it will to be to give that up…" He dodged the swat she aimed at his chest. "I can't wait. You do realize we'll need to christen every room, right."

She merely smiled. "Some more than once."

"Jesus, you're already married. Feel free to stop with all the mushy shit." Waylen joined them at the bar, Presley on his arm. She was only just starting to show, but Waylen enjoyed teasing her about how she wouldn't be able to see her toes, soon.

Kian waved him off. "I can't help it if I'm so damn sexy the lady can't keep her hands off me."

"The lady's crazy." Porter joined them at the counter, looking more than a bit unsettled. "Do you know how close to the volcano she took me on the way over? The woman's insane."

Blake merely shrugged. "Those geologists wanted more photos. I don't make up the assignments. I simply fly the helicopter."

"Insanely. You fly the helicopter insanely, Blake." Porter tugged on his jacket. "So, this place is finally the team bar. I love the new turtle logo as the O in Ohana's."

Kian beamed. "Blake had that made for us. A thank you for helping her out with Russo even though we told her she didn't owe us, anything."

"I owe you far more, but the sign's a start." Blake raised her brow at Porter. "So, who was the blonde I saw you chatting up outside? I seem to recall she's been in here before. Like every time you've been here for the past month."

Porter didn't so much as smile. "Someone not involved with Henry Russo, the Marshal Service, or any form of organized crime." He ordered two beers. "And if you ask me any more questions, I'll arrest you."

"So, she's special. Got it."

"You are such a pain in my ass. Let me know when it's karaoke time. I might be drunk enough to give it a go."

Blake leaned over as Porter joined the blonde Blake had mentioned at a secluded table in the corner. "You guys can run a check on her, right? I don't want anyone messing with Porter."

Waylen snorted. "I'm pretty sure Porter runs background checks on everyone. He's as paranoid as Harlan."

"I'm not paranoid, I'm cautious." Harlan sidled up to the bar, ordering more beer for his table. "And I already ran a background check on Porter's friend. She's a paralegal at that new law firm. Doesn't have so much as a parking ticket on her record. Her father's a cop, so… I think they might actually have a shot."

"Have Raider and Piper found a place, yet?"

Harlan chuckled. "She's got a pretty substantial list of must-haves. I think they'll be looking for a while, yet. Not that Raider seems to mind. He's as lovesick as Kian."

Kian swatted Harlan with the end of a towel. "I'm a happily married man, now."

"Yeah, a lovesick one."

Blake leaned back over and kissed him, again. "Don't listen to him. You're gorgeous."

He kissed her, ignoring the comments his buddies tossed his way because there was nothing better than having Blake touching him. Whatever way he could manage.

She wiped her thumb across his mouth once they'd parted. "Can you keep my helmet and the folder behind the bar? Us girls are going to take a turn singing."

"Anything for you, sweetheart."

The way she blushed… It was as if he'd lifted all that darkness she'd been drowning in. Brought her back into the light.

Blake slid off the seat, took a few steps, then darted back over, dragging him down for one more drugging kiss. "There's a surprise in the folder. In case you want to have a look."

Kian arched a brow as she skipped off, hooking her arm through Presley's as they grabbed the other ladies — made their way to the stage.

Waylen coughed. "That didn't sound ominous, at all."

Kian opened the folder, lifting an envelope off the stack of documents. It felt heavy. Definitely more than just paper inside.

A quick slice of a knife, and he had the side open — was able to shake out a small picture frame. He turned it over, staring at some weird image that looked vaguely human only amidst some kind of snowstorm. He read the note stuck to the glass. "Looks like Waylen was right, after all."

He paused, letting all the words sink in before he all but dropped the damn thing, looking over at Blake. She smiled at him, inhaling when he vaulted over the bar, quickly closing the distance before lifting her up — swinging her around.

She grasped his shoulders, kissing him again when he pulled her in close. "So, I assume you're okay with the new development?"

"Okay, I'm... fuck, I don't know what to say. You..."

This kiss was carnal. Enough that everyone started hooting. Telling them to get a room, but he didn't care. Would take all the ribbing because she was his.

Blake palmed his jaw. "We'll talk after. I just couldn't keep it a secret any longer. Now, go... We've got some serious songs to butcher."

Kian gave her ass a swat, knowing she'd get him back later as he returned to the bar, shaking his buddies' hands as they passed the photo around.

Waylen held out his hand. "I believe you owe me fifty bucks."

Kian shoved his hand away. "For what?"

"For being wrong."

Kian shook his head but handed the guy a few bills. "You're an ass, you know that?"

"A rich one."

Kian glanced over at Lane. "So, you and Cassie thinking about kids?"

Lane laughed. "We just got married. One milestone at a time. Besides, you and Waylen seem to be having enough for all of us."

"Tick tock, my friend."

"Shut up." Lane pointed at Harlan and Raider. "Let the rest of the team make it official, then I'll start thinking about kids."

Waylen snorted. "Wanna put fifty bucks on that?"

Lane gave him a side eye, still sipping on his beer, when he motioned toward a table off to the side. "I've been meaning to ask, who's the reserved table for?"

Kian frowned. "I don't know. It was like that when I got here."

He waved Raider over, nodding at the reserved sign sitting in the center. "Who are the VIPs?"

Raider shrugged. "No idea. Hawk asked if I'd set a table aside for him. Something about a training team coming in tonight."

"A training team?"

"To be honest, I don't think Hawk knows much about them, either. Apparently, this came directly from Hank. Some favor for an old friend. But why don't you ask Blake? She might have more intel since she flew them in."

"Blake flew them in with Porter?"

Kian looked over at Blake, wondering how much longer their song would be, when the door opened, again, a few large silhouettes filling the doorway. Four men shuffled in, scanning the place, and there was no missing the telltale look in their eyes. The ones Kian knew he and his team shared. That spoke of hard decisions and ugly memories.

They glanced over at the bar, eyes widening before their mouths kicked into a hint of a smile.

Kian shook his head, slapping Waylen on the back as he nodded at Lane and Raider. "Well, I'll be damned. Talk about a small world. Look who just walked in."

WALKER'S MISSION

BROTHERHOOD PROTECTORS WORLD

TEAM EAGLE
BOOK 10

KRIS NORRIS

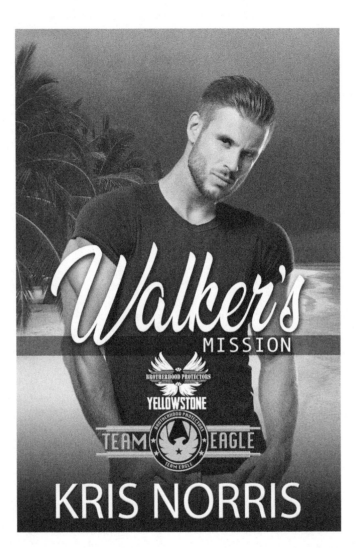

Walker's
MISSION

BROTHERHOOD PROTECTORS
YELLOWSTONE

TEAM EAGLE

KRIS NORRIS

EXCERPT ~ WALKER'S MISSION

"You're kidding, right?"

Walker Pierce looked at the guy sitting next to him in the cockpit — Booker Hayes. Fellow Flight Concepts' pilot, and the man Walker was sure had lost his mind. Because Walker could have sworn Booker had just announced Walker and Xavier were going to have an old-fashioned dogfight.

Well, as much as two helicopters could dogfight.

Booker grinned. "I thought you'd be excited."

"And I thought we were up here to get this stupid proficiency check over with."

Not that Walker didn't approve of them, but it was the second one since he'd become a participating member of Team Eagle and the Brotherhood Protector's Aviation Division in West Yellowstone.

Booker shrugged. "I know having to jump through all these hoops, again, is a pain, but I understand why Hank wants us all to have our checks due in the summer. However, since we're signing off on each other, I thought... why not have a bit of fun?"

"And a dogfight equates to fun?"

"Please. I don't need to sit here, ticking off all these boxes. You've been flying for twenty years — most of that with Flight Concepts. And after all the tours and equipment you flew in the service, this is pretty vanilla. So, let's up the ante, a bit."

Walker laughed. "I've forgotten how nuts you really are, buddy. But before we get this party started, are you sure Xavier's up for it? I mean, the guy's good, but..."

But he hadn't spent all those years flying special forces into enemy territory. Hadn't learned how to pilot multiple foreign aircraft, or how to avoid the most advanced tracking systems.

Hadn't been behind the controls on that godforsaken mission that had landed them all here.

Booker grinned. "He seems to think we're antiquated. That he's got a leg up because he's younger — more savvy, I guess."

"Is that so? Well, let's put that theory to the test." Walker thumbed at Corbin River sitting in the back. "I assume that's why the kid's along?"

"He's our gunner. We've got laser targeting sensors placed around the exterior. Whoever lights them all up, first, wins. Unless you're worried Corbin doesn't have it in him."

A huff sounded across the comms. "You jerks know I can hear you, right?"

Booker twisted in his seat until he was looking into the back. "Yup."

Corbin snorted. "Now, I know why Callie's always calling you an ass."

"Gretta calls you worse than that, so…"

"That, she does." Corbin waited until Walker gave him a quick side eye. "So, old man. We gonna do this, or what?"

"Again, I'm only ten years older than you."

"And still like a father figure."

Walker laughed. Corbin wasn't wrong. Walker did have more of a mentor relationship with the guy than simply being a best friend. Not full-on father, but he couldn't deny he had an innate need to nurture the kid. Something that had developed over the course of their extended rehab together when Corbin had struggled with losing his career before he'd even turned thirty. And Walker wouldn't change their dynamic, even if the kid did see him as old. Hell, with all Walker had experienced in the service, he felt ancient, sometimes.

Except when he was with Blair Hughes — MI6

agent and Gretta's sister. Blair made him feel like a lovesick teenager — one destined to slowly going insane because Walker had absolutely no idea how to move beyond friendship with her. And it was from more than just his lack of experience in that department. The fact he'd never been in love — had never wanted that kind of entanglement in his life, before. Sure, he'd had his share of lovers, and if sex was all he was interested in, he would have done everything he could to have charmed Blair into his bed.

But for the first time in his life, he wanted more. And he had a bad feeling his inability to wrap his head around how to initiate that next move, stemmed from something deeper. Something he feared was linked to fate. Or maybe faith.

But how could he take a leap of faith when that faith had been thoroughly shattered, along with the right side of his body? And he wasn't convinced the doctors had put it all back together. That, some-where along the way, they'd lost a few pieces — the important ones. And he was left searching for bits of his soul he doubted he'd ever find.

Blair had changed that. Filled in the empty spaces. A fact that had him questioning if the real reason he was stuck cruising in the friend zone was because somewhere deep inside, he didn't believe he deserved to be happy — to live. But he knew if he didn't decide which side of the fence he was on soon, he'd lose far more than those replacement parts she'd given him.

He'd lose his one chance at finding forever.

Booker cleared his throat, giving Walker a raise of his brow. "Well? You ready?"

Walker groaned inwardly. He'd been getting lost in thought frequently since the accident. The one constant it seemed. Thankfully, Booker understood, better than anyone, how Walker felt. The guilt. The sense of failure. And his buddy rarely called him on it.

Walker admired the way Booker had seemingly put that accident behind him. Maybe not completely, but ever since he'd reunited with Callie Jensen, ex-DEA agent and Booker's new wife, the guy had definitely achieved more of a Zen quality regarding that failed op. The kind of calm Walker strived for but couldn't quite attain.

He snorted, rolling his right shoulder to loosen the tension that seeped into all the screws and plates holding everything together, then smiled. "I hope Xavier's ego isn't too delicate because the man's about to get schooled."

Booked grinned, gave Xavier the green light over the radio, then nodded at the control panel. "All right, Walker. Let's see how far you can push this baby before she breaks."

Corbin coughed. "Wait, Walker. You're not actually going to break… Shit."

Walker tipped the machine forward, gaining some speed before banking hard to the left. He got a bead on Xavier as the guy slipped in behind him, shadowing his movements. But if Xavier thought Walker was going to make it this fight easy, the man was in for one hell of a ride.

Walker slowed, allowing Xavier to close the distance just a bit before he peeled off — pegged the machine at some insane speed as he headed for the tree line. No fancy zigzagging, no hesitation. Just the nose aimed at the pines, and the wind whistling through the cockpit.

Ten seconds in, and they were screaming — quickly eating up the air between the chopper and the trees. Another five, and he had the machine tipped over as he skimmed the tops, the blades just missing the branches. Needles whizzed past the bubble, the occasional leaf fluttering against the plexiglass before flying off.

Corbin muttered something in the back, but Walker ignored it. This was his calling. Regardless of how the accident had affected him — the nightmares and flashbacks he pushed aside — this was still the one place he felt in control. Where, for as long as the flight lasted, he believed he was enough.

A blast of static sounded over the radio before laughter filled the cockpit. "Jesus, Walker. You don't have to go completely insane. It's only a game."

Xavier. Though, Walker wasn't buying the

casual tone. The guy was more than competitive, and Walker knew it.

He chuckled, dropping them into an opening in the trees before snaking his way along a river. "It's never just a game, buddy. Regardless, it's one I intend to win. Catch me if you can."

He clicked off the mic, then activated the internal comms. "Corbin, please tell me Xavier is above us and off to the right."

Corbin snorted. "Nailed it. He's counting on you following this river."

"And we will… for a bit."

Walker kept the bird low, swinging her back and forth around the tight bends, all the while sensing Xavier following him. Staying on his six but waiting until Walker was forced to climb to initiate any kind of attack. What would make Xavier's positioning ideal, except Walker wasn't going to climb the way the other man thought. In fact, he planned on going on the offensive.

A few more bends, then Walker was banking her over. Not quite rolling her as he climbed and reversed his direction, but as close as he could get while maintaining positive G's. What would prevent the blades from simply shooting off. He finished nearly level with Xavier's machine, his chopper on a collision course, still going that insane speed.

Not the typical game of chicken, but it counted. And Walker hadn't lost a round, yet.

Xavier held on longer than Walker had figured, dodging right at the last moment. And that was all the opening Walker needed.

He peeled over, nearly rolling her, again, while opening up Corbin's side. "Hey, kid. Pull yourself up off the floor and show us what you've got."

Corbin mumbled something about how Walker was certifiable, and that he wasn't sure he wanted to fly with him, anymore, before shouldering his weapon.

He took a couple of seconds to gauge his trajectory, then fired. Lighting up four of the laser targets on Xavier's helicopter.

Xavier countered, diving down as he banked the machine hard to the left, coming up behind Walker when he had to ease back to avoid getting too close to a few outcrops. And skimming the side of the moutain would have definitely had Walker crossing over to the other side of crazy when it really was just a game. But he hadn't been joking. He'd failed once. He wasn't about to fail, again, real or not.

Xavier's gunner got off a few shots, activating one of the targets. Nothing close to ending the game, but Walker vowed it was the only hit the other team would get.

He headed for a narrow pass between two outcrops. More of a long chasm, really, just large enough to sneak through. He held the machine steady, dismissing Corbin's rough inhale that sounded over the comms. True, it was probably a bit risky for a training mission, but Walker knew, first-hand, that if he didn't push himself here and now, he'd back down when their lives really were on the line. And he'd sworn he'd hang up his wings long before that happened.

Twenty feet back, and Xavier was talking over the radio — telling Walker it was too dangerous. That he should back down. Some bullshit about not dying. But Walker had already faced death, and compared to the accident on the aircraft carrier, this was that vanilla crap Booker had been talking about.

A few more feet, and Walker had the machine tipped over — was skimming it through the open-ing. It only took a few seconds to squeeze the chopper through, but it felt longer. Minutes. Hell, hours with the rock walls looming in close, only a few feet between the sides of the chasm and the machine. What could have easily killed them if he'd lost his concentration or worse, his nerve.

Screaming out the other side intact had him grinning, nodding at Booker when the guy shouted, "Hell, yeah," into the comms. Walker chanced a glance back at Corbin, but the kid merely glared at him, shaking his head before chuckling.

Corbin shouldered his weapon, again. "Jackass. Stop patting yourself on the back for not killing us, and get me in position so I can hit those last sensors."

Walker banked the chopper to the right, dropping over the top of one outcrop and into a valley on the other side. "Don't get snarky because you didn't get all six when I practically served Xavier up on a platter for you."

"I went four for four."

Walker shrugged. "And yet, there're still two left."

"Is that your way of saying you can only line his chopper up once?"

"Oh, how you'll eat those words." Walker followed the rocky hill around to the right, popping out behind Xavier's machine, just like he'd hoped. "This close enough for you, or should I get *lover* close like you and Gretta?"

"Just hold it steady, wise ass."

Two shots, two hits, as the last remaining sensors lit up, signaling a win.

Corbin snorted. "You were saying…"

"An ace would've only needed one shot."

"And, if we were using bullets, I could have bounced one."

Walker laughed. "Fine. I guess you haven't lost too much, after all. I was getting worried for a moment. Thought maybe Gretta had brought you over to the dark side. Had you throwing as many shots at a problem as possible instead of finessing it."

"I'm going to tell her you said that and see just how savvy she can be with a rifle aimed at your ass. Betting she'll only need one bullet, old man."

Walker raised one hand. "Easy there, kid. I'm not ashamed to admit Gretta scares me, just a bit."

A blast of static sounded through the cockpit followed by a long sigh. "I take back all the things I ever said about Booker because Walker, you are hands down, the craziest pilot I've ever known. I can't believe you actually flew through that crack."

Walker laughed. "It was a sizeable gap, and you do realize you just challenged Booker to a dogfight, right Xavier?"

"Oh, no. I didn't—"

"Oh, yes, you did." Booker nodded at Walker as he took ahold of the controls on his side of the machine. "It's my turn. So, reset those targets, brother. I'll give you sixty seconds head start, then, the hunt is on."

It was only a couple hours before sunset when the men finally called it quits, joking and shoving each other as they walked across the helipad and headed for their vehicles. Somehow, they'd managed to conveniently forget they were late for a gathering at Booker and Callie's house. Though, Walker had a feeling Booker had subconsciously planned it that way. That he knew Walker still didn't do well in large groups, where the prospect of the carrier accident was bound to surface. And he'd be left backpedaling, trying to brush off any comments about how he'd done well saving as many lives as he had. That somehow, he wasn't to blame.

That his greatest failure had earned him a medal.

Booker understood. Had a similar velvet-lined box stashed somewhere in his house, gathering dust.

Corbin jumped into the passenger side of Walker's truck, motioning to the road. "You gonna get this baby rolling, or are we going to sit here and wait until everyone's too drunk to get under your skin?"

Walker shook his head. "Why are we best friends, again?"

"Because no one else can stand you."

"Jackass."

"Drive, grandpa."

"Now, you're pushing it."

Corbin grinned, dodging the swing Walker aimed at his shoulder, mumbling something about Walker being too slow, before Walker revved the engine then headed out. Corbin understood Walker's reservations, too. Which was why the kid was joking around. Goading him so Walker would forget about his demons long enough to enjoy the barbecue. Especially if Blair was there.

Which she should be, unless Gretta had decided the guys were taking too long and had dragged her sister off to the gun range. Walker wasn't sure how a Brit had developed such a passion for weapons, but there was no denying both sisters excelled at their jobs. Even if the prospect of Blair heading back to London gutted him.

Of course, he hadn't exactly given her a reason to stay. Instead, he'd spent the past five months agonizing over the fact he was out of his element — had fallen for her without even realizing it until the prospect of it ending before it had even begun was slapping him in the face. He should have been showing her there were viable options for her, right here, in West Yellowstone. That Gretta wasn't the only person hoping she'd stay.

Sure, Blair had been recovering, at first, from a gunshot wound she'd sustained when she'd uncovered a mole inside MI6 and had sent Gretta a series of cryptic texts. What had gotten Corbin and Walker intertwined with Blair, to begin with. But she'd recovered enough Walker could have asked her out long before now. The fact her medical leave was quickly coming to a close was proof that he'd been stalling.

More regrets he could add to his list.

Corbin didn't talk during the short drive from the hanger to Booker's place, simply staring out the window until Walker had parked his truck as far back as possible. His failsafe in case the noise and the people got to him, and he needed to make a quick exit.

That, or if he was able to convince Blair to go for a long drive to stargaze. What might be the perfect opportunity to finally make his move.

Corbin shook his head, glancing at the driveway snaking off in front of them. "Still parking in the back nine, huh."

Walker shrugged. "The walk is good rehab for your back."

"Pretty damn sure it's not my back you're thinking about." Corbin arched a brow. "Is this so you can make a quick getaway if everyone starts talking about the aircraft carrier incident, or so you can finally grow a set and spirit Blair away?"

"Shut up."

Corbin grabbed Walker's arm when he tried to step out. "I realize we're all still dealing with that day. And I'm the last person who'll ever tell you to just get over it. I know the toll it's taken. The guilt and blame. But you're better when you're with Blair. You know that, right?"

"It's—"

"Not complicated. You're stupid in love with her, and she's smart, but somehow equally stupid in love with you."

"Whoa. We're not even dating, so pull back on the whole 'love' thing. We're friends." He swallowed the bitter aftertaste of the lie as the words formed on his tongue, doing his best to push forward. "Close friends, but…"

"You've spent the past few months practically glued at the hip. Just because you haven't actually made it to a bed doesn't mean your feelings aren't real. And before you start listing all the ways I'm full of shit, I've had a front-row seat, as has Gretta."

Walker glanced at Booker's home off in the distance, rolling his right shoulder to ease the tension that had crept into it as soon as Corbin had called him out. "I care."

"Walker." Corbin waited until he made eye contact. "Why is it so hard for you to admit you're crazy about her? I realize this is uncharted territory for you — that whole bullshit *love is like a pizza* analogy you once gave me, and how *bad pizza can stick with you for life*. But you just flew a chopper through a freaking crack in the mountains. Admitting you're in love with Blair seems pretty benign by comparison."

He closed his eyes for a moment, willing the anxious roll in his stomach to ease. "This has nothing to do with uncharted territory or crashing and burning."

"Then, what?" Corbin narrowed his eyes, glancing at the entrance to Booker's backyard. "The accident?"

"Ignoring the fact a dozen soldiers lost their careers that day, there were eight men who never made it out of those two choppers alive because of me. And yeah, I know. The machine failed. It wasn't really my fault. I followed protocol, but..." He stared down at his hands, hating the way they shook. "How is it remotely okay that I have the chance to be with someone as amazing as Blair when they..."

The truck fell silent, nothing but the weight of his words hanging in the air between them. The truth he still hadn't come to terms with — might never come to terms with because he was alive, and they weren't.

Corbin finally sighed, opened the door, then stepped out. He made his way around to Walker's side, leaning against the front panel as Walker slipped out of the vehicle. "If you want to spend the rest of your life seeking the kind of redemption you can't possibly find, I won't stop you. And if you want to let Blair slip away back to London because you don't think you deserve to be happy — to have a life beyond work — I'll keep my mouth shut."

He pushed off the truck and started down the gravel driveway, pausing several feet out as he glanced back over his shoulder. "But you might want to look around at some of those *casualties* you seem to think you caused because the rest of us are fine. Sure, our lives are different, but that doesn't automatically equate to them being worse. Look at me. If I hadn't been on that damn chopper —

hadn't lost what I thought would be the rest of my life — I never would have found Gretta. And it might sound cliché, but I wouldn't trade a lifetime's worth of missions for the next fifty years with her. Which is crazy because I never thought I'd have a family until I was an old man... like you."

He stared as Corbin continued down the driveway, disappearing behind a row of trucks. Shouts and hoots sounded in the distance followed by music drifting along the breeze.

Because the rest of us are fine...

He hadn't really thought about it that way. Hadn't stopped long enough to really take stock — realize that, while Corbin was right and everyone's lives were different, his teammates weren't unhappy. Weren't moping around, lost in their own horrors. In fact, Walker was the only one that seemed stuck in the past, afraid to move on.

He wanted to move on. Wanted more than just missions and training to occupy the hours. To have the kind of future his teammates were creating.

And he wanted it with Blair.

He just didn't know how to bury the memories. Silence the screams and cries that echoed inside his head whenever he let his guard down. To look in the mirror and not see what the wreckage had left behind. And it was more than the scars and the metal holding him together. It was the men he'd left on the carrier's deck. Their faces. Their pain.

Their sacrifice.

And despite everything Corbin had said, Walker wasn't sure he could push it all aside. That he could be the guy he pretended to be when his teammates were watching. The one who never backed down. Who flew a chopper without hesitation or fear.

If it was possible to be anyone other than Walker Pierce — the man who'd failed.

OTHER BOOKS BY KRIS NORRIS

SINGLES

CENTERFOLD

KEEPING FAITH

IRON WILL

MY SOUL TO KEEP

RICOCHET

ROPE'S END

SERIES

'TIL DEATH

1 - DEADLY VISION

2 - DEADLY OBSESSION

3 - DEADLY DECEPTION

BROTHERHOOD PROTECTORS ~ Elle James

1 - MIDNIGHT RANGER

2 – CARVED IN ICE

3 - GOING IN BLIND

2 - TWICE BITTEN

3 - BLOOD OF THE WOLF

ENCHANTED LOVERS

1 - HEALING HANDS

FROM GRACE

1 - GABRIEL

2 – MICHAEL

THRESHOLD

1 - GRAVE MEASURES

TOMBSTONE

1 - MARSHAL LAW

2 - FORGOTTEN

3 - LAST STAND

WAYWARD SOULS

1 - DELTA FORCE: CANNON

2 - DELTA FORCE: COLT

3 - DELTA FORCE: SIX

4 - DELTA FORCE: CROW

5 - DELTA FORCE: PHOENIX

COLLECTIONS

BLUE COLLAR COLLECTION

DARK PROPHECY: VOL 1

INTO THE SPIRIT, BOXED SET

COMING SOON

DELTA FORCE: FETCH

TEAM KOA — BRAVO

ABOUT KRIS NORRIS

Author, single mother, slave to chaos—she's a jack-of-all-trades who's constantly looking for her ever elusive clone.

Kris loves connecting with fellow book enthusiasts. You can find her on these social media platforms…

krisnorris.ca
contactme@krisnorris.ca

 facebook.com/kris.norris.731
 instagram.com/girlnovelist
 amazon.com/author/krisnorris

BROTHERHOOD PROTECTORS WORLD

ORIGINAL SERIES BY ELLE JAMES

Brotherhood Protectors Hawaii World

Team Koa Alpha

Lane Unleashed - Regan Black

Harlan Unleashed - Stacey Wilk

Raider Unleashed - Lori Matthews

Waylen Unleashed - Jen Talty

Kian Unleashed - Kris Norris

Brotherhood Protectors Yellowstone World

Team Wolf

Guarding Harper - - Desiree Holt

Guarding Hannah - Delilah Devlin

Guarding Eris - Reina Torres

Guarding Payton - Jen Talty

Guarding Leah - Regan Black

Team Eagle

Booker's Mission - Kris Norris

Hunter's Mission - Kendall Talbot

Gunn's Mission - Delilah Devlin

Xavier's Mission - Lori Matthews

Wyatt's Mission - Jen Talty

Corbin's Mission - Jen Talty

Tyson's Mission - Delilah Devlin

Knox's Mission - Barb Han

Colton's Mission - Kendall Talbot

Walker's Mission - Kris Norris

Brotherhood Protectors Colorado World
Team Watchdog

Mason's Watch - Jen Talty

Asher's Watch - Leanne Tyler

Cruz's Watch - Stacey Wilk

Kent's Watch- Deanna L. Rowley

Ryder's Watch- Kris Norris

Team Raptor

Darius' Promise - Jen Talty

Simon's Promise - Leanne Tyler

Nash's Promise - Stacey Wilk

Spencer's Promise - Deanna L. Rowley

Logan's Promise - Kris Norris

Team Falco

Fighting for Esme - Jen Talty

Fighting for Charli - Leanne Tyler

Fighting for Tessa - Stacey Wilk

Fighting for Kora - Deanna L. Rowley

Fighting for Fiona - Kris Norris

Athena Project

Beck's Six - Desiree Holt

Victoria's Six - Delilah Devlin

Cygny's Six - Reina Torres

Fay's Six - Jen Talty

Melody's Six - Regan Black

Team Trojan

Defending Sophie - Desiree Holt

Defending Evangeline - Delilah Devlin

Defending Casey - Reina Torres

Defending Sparrow - Jen Talty

Defending Avery - Regan Black

BROTHERHOOD PROTECTORS
ORIGINAL SERIES BY ELLE JAMES

Brotherhood Protectors International

Athens Affair (#1)

Belgian Betrayal (#2)

Croatia Collateral (#3)

Dublin Debacle (#4)

Edinburgh Escape (#5)

Brotherhood Protectors Hawaii

Kalea's Hero (#1)

Leilani's Hero (#2)

Kiana's Hero (#3)

Maliea's Hero (#4)

Emi's Hero (#5)

Sachie's Hero (#6)

Kimo's Hero (#7)

Alana's Hero (#8)

Nala's Hero (#9)

Mika's Hero (#10)

Bayou Brotherhood Protectors

Remy (#1)

Gerard (#2)

Lucas (#3)

Beau (#4)

Rafael (#5)

Valentin (#6)

Landry (#7)

Simon (#8)

Maurice (#9)

Jacques (#10)

Brotherhood Protectors Yellowstone

Saving Kyla (#1)

Saving Chelsea (#2)

Saving Amanda (#3)

Saving Liliana (#4)

Saving Breely (#5)

Saving Savvie (#6)

Saving Jenna (#7)

Saving Peyton (#8)

Saving Londyn (#9)

Brotherhood Protectors Colorado

Brotherhood Protectors

ABOUT ELLE JAMES

ELLE JAMES also writing as MYLA JACKSON is a *New York Times* and *USA Today* Bestselling author of books including cowboys, intrigues and paranormal adventures that keep her readers on the edges of their seats. When she's not at her computer, she's traveling, snow skiing, boating, or riding her ATV, dreaming up new stories. Learn more about Elle James at www.ellejames.com

Website | Facebook | Twitter | GoodReads | Newsletter | BookBub | Amazon

Or visit her alter ego Myla Jackson at
mylajackson.com
Website | Facebook | Twitter | Newsletter

Follow Me!
www.ellejames.com
ellejamesauthor@gmail.com

Made in the USA
Coppell, TX
31 October 2024

39415647R10174